A native of Brixham in Devon, England, Richard Dee left Devon in his teens and travelled the world in the Merchant Navy, qualifying as a Master Mariner in 1986. Coming ashore to be with his growing family, he flirted with various jobs, including dockmaster, insurance surveyor and port control officer, finally becoming a Thames pilot over twenty years ago. He regularly took vessels of all sizes through the Thames Barrier and upriver as far as London Bridge. He recently returned to live in Brixham, where he has taken up food writing and blogging. He retired from pilotage in 2015 to start an organic bakery, supplying local shops and cafés. *Ribbonworld* is his first paperback novel with SilverWood Books; he has previously self-published two science-fiction stories, available electronically. He is married with three adult children.

GN00600726

Enjoy

RIBBONWORLD

RICHARD DEE

SilverWood

Published in 2015 by SilverWood Books

SilverWood Books Ltd
14 Small Street, Bristol, BS1 1DE, United Kingdom
www.silverwoodbooks.co.uk

ISBN 978-1-78132-467-7 (paperback)
ISBN 978-1-78132-468-4 (ebook)

British Library Cataloguing in Publication Data
A CIP catalogue record for this book is available from
the British Library

Set in Sabon by SilverWood Books
Printed on responsibly sourced paper

For Fran, with thanks

1

The door hissed shut behind me and I dropped my bags and flexed my fingers. I was on the fourth floor and the lift wasn't working, something about a safety inspection. So I had used the stairs. After nearly two days sitting around in space, my legs were trembling with the effort and I wheezed like an eighty-year-old with asthma. I was hot from the effort and the sweat dripped off my nose. I wiped my forehead with my palm, leaving a damp patch on my trouser leg where my hand rested. The ventilator was making a noise not unlike a cement mixer, filling the room with freezing cold air and making the dust sparkle in the harsh lighting. The cold air cooled my sweat-soaked shirt and made me shiver.

A typical cheap hotel room lay before me; with its familiar layout and standard colour scheme it could have been anywhere. The carpet was worn and threadbare and looking down I could see that it didn't quite reach into one corner. These hotel rooms were mass produced with the furniture installed and shipped in packs; you only had to bolt them together around a metal frame and seal the edges. All the services were pre-installed; after plugging in the electricity and water they were ready to go. At least that meant that I knew where the thermostat was. I reached across and dialled it to minimum. The noise decreased.

Hotels like these were mainly used by manual workers on short term contracts, who were always so tired that they didn't care where they stopped as long as it had a bed and a supply of beer. I was here because it was cheap and anonymous. And I wanted to stretch my budget.

The furniture was all made of fibreboard; the shiny surface layer that was supposed to look like wood but didn't was chipped at the edges. The bed at least was inviting, although that may have been due to the fact that I hadn't slept for thirty-six hours. I should have been here yesterday, but a magnetic storm had made us waste a day in high orbit.

We had spent the time strapped into the hard seats on a shuttle; the liner had departed, taking with it the relative comforts of deep space travel. Normally you spent a maximum of a couple of hours in a shuttle; they had the oxygen for much longer, of course, regulations demanded it, but regulations didn't say anything about comfort. And on a personal level I had a thing about vacuum. The liner was built to disguise it but the shuttle was less able to hide the fact that I was only a couple of sheets of metal away from a whole lot of nothing.

With a sinking feeling I realised that I could have been in any of the cheap hotels I had ever stopped in. And I've stopped in a few recently. In fact my life had been on a downward spiral for a while; work and money had dried up and I was scratching a living on jobs that an intern could handle. Trouble was, the interns were getting the better jobs and I was left in places like this.

There was a short narrow corridor from the doorway, with the bathroom on the right-hand side. This led into the main part of the room. Straight ahead was a large picture window, with stained curtains covering the view. A desk, a chair and the end of the bed were the only visible furnishings. I couldn't see it from here, but I knew that there was a closet against the bathroom wall.

I caught my reflection in the chipped mirror. Not glass – it would never survive in a place like this – but unbreakable polymer. It had warped a little; I looked back at myself with a strangely hunched body, wearing worn and crumpled clothes and with unruly hair just a touch longer than fashionable. My excuse was that it was my reaction to the prison haircut. Below it was a distorted face, with two days' stubble and the slightly perplexed expression of someone who was having trouble coming to terms with a fall from grace. Unfortunately, the expression wasn't due to the warped mirror, but a fact of my recent life. My fall had been two years ago but it still felt like yesterday.

I needed to get in touch with my contact; he must have been wondering where I had got to. I'd sent him a text message from orbit to say that I would be late, but of course I hadn't known how long I would be. I checked my phone again; he hadn't replied. I hoped he hadn't changed his mind – I was on a fixed fee, so the quicker I got finished and left, the better. At least I had my return ticket, so I could always get off of this rock.

But first, I needed a drink. Not necessarily alcoholic, just as long as it was wet it would do the job. The shuttles have toilets but it's a performance in low gravity and with fourteen on board the shuttle it had soon become unpleasant so I had tried to avoid the need as much as possible. And now I was thirsty. In these rooms there was usually a fridge in the corner between the desk and the window, stocked with refreshments. The fridge was there all right but somewhat predictably it was empty. I sighed; the contents had probably already been added to my bill. A glass of water from the bathroom would have to do.

My breathing had just about returned to normal as I waved my hand over the sensor to open the bathroom door. The light turned green and the door started to slide. There must have been something jamming the trackway, as it only opened an inch or so, then stopped and slid shut with a thump. Strange. I tried it again.

This time it went a little further and I could see a mirror

in front of me. I tried to put my head into the gap but the door didn't open far enough for the light to switch itself on. I couldn't see what was stopping it. It slid shut again as I ducked back out of the way.

There was not enough room for me to get in and anyway I didn't fancy getting stuck in there so I called the desk on the internal phone. In an emergency I'm handy enough with the technology, and I knew that all the electronics were in a panel by the door. But I would probably need a special passkey to get in without causing any damage. Not only that, my bill might suffer. It wasn't an emergency so it was easier to call.

The bored voice of the desk clerk that I had met on the way in told me that someone would be along; this wasn't the sort of place that had a man poised to cater for the guests' whims so I would have to wait. I put the phone down and started to unpack, first placing my valuables in the safe under the desk.

I shut the door and set the lock to my thumbprint. Then I unzipped my bag and opened the closet door. At least this one opened, and I saw that the previous occupant had left a jacket in there. It was a classy piece of cloth, by a designer that I used to know socially, and looked about my size. I had owned clothing like this before, but in my present circumstances I could never have afforded one like it. After about a second, I decided that it was coming with me. If I gave it in at the desk, whoever was on duty would probably keep it, so the owner would never see it again either way. My luck might be changing. I hung my stuff in front of it, hiding it behind my cheap copies.

I had a wait, so I thought that I'd just lie down for a moment on the bed. I rolled onto the thin, lumpy mattress and was almost instantly asleep.

I was back on my yacht, a forty-foot ceramic hulled cruiser called *True Story*. We were anchored off one of the Jigsaw Islands on Centra; it was a warm, cloudless day, the sun shining on a calm sea and there was laughter and wine and happiness with a crowd of people. The barbeque was producing steaks and prawns and there was a trestle table on the poop groaning with good food, served by a white-clad steward. People were jumping into the water and swimming around the hull, having a good time at my expense. But I didn't care because I knew they were my friends.

I looked over to the stern platform and saw Gaynor climb back on board. She was as sleek as an otter, her long hair, orange this week, plastered to her face and shoulders. As she walked towards me she dripped liquid diamonds on the hardwood deck. She came and put her arm round my waist and I felt the heat beneath the damp as our hips touched. "Come on, Miles," she whispered in my ear. "Let's get rid of this lot."

The scene dissolved and I was answering a knock at my door, back at my apartment. I opened it to the grim faces and uniforms saying, "Mr Goram, will you come with us." It was raining and a small crowd watched as I was led, handcuffed, into the police car. I could hear the excited whispers as the cameras were waved in my face, flashes blinding me.

Next I heard the words, "Guilty as charged; I sentence you to five years' imprisonment." They echoed around the empty courtroom, just me and the prosecutor and the guards.

"It's a set-up!" I screamed.

"Take him away," said the prosecutor.

Then the bare metal of the cell door slammed shut behind me and I pounded on it.

The door buzzer woke me with a jolt. Looking at my watch I saw that I had been asleep for almost an hour. "Coming," I called, thinking it must be the repair man. I was feeling a bit disorientated from the dream so I didn't look through the spy-hole, I just pushed the lock release by the door and stood back.

The door slid open and there were two of them, in crumpled looking suits and wearing worn expressions. I could tell straight away that they weren't repair men.

"Who are you?" the taller one said, waving an official-looking card at me. His gaze travelled over my shoulder, taking it all in. I had déjà-vu; this was just like it had been in my dream, and before that in my reality.

"I could ask you the same," I replied, suddenly very awake.

"We're the police," said the second man, shorter and more rotund, with dark hair and a beard, "Detectives Flanagan and Chumna. We got a tip-off."

I had a sinking feeling. "I didn't call you, I called the desk – I can't get the bathroom door open."

They came into the room as I backed down the corridor; the one called Flanagan took a small multi-driver from his inside pocket and levered open the control panel for the room electronics. He fiddled around for a while, and the bathroom door started to slide open. When it reached the obstruction, it didn't shut; it stopped with a six-inch gap.

The motor kept whirring as the two detectives put latex gloves on and held the edge of the door. They both pulled, grunting with the effort. Whatever was in there wasn't giving up easily. Slowly the door slid open until Chumna was able to squeeze through the gap. He disappeared. There was a dragging sound and the door opened fully.

The light came on, just as he called out, "Barry, get in here."

Flanagan disappeared into the room. "Don't come in," he called to me over his shoulder. Fair enough, but by going to the open door I could see what was going on in the mirror. And I was still enough of a journalist to be nosey.

A man's body was lying in the shower stall, with one leg flung out against the door. He was about my size, early middle aged and muscular, his flesh slackened in death.

There was no blood, or obvious wound, but as my gaze travelled over his body, I saw that the neck was mottled with blue and black bruises, below light stubble.

His eyes held my gaze, open wide, bulging from the skull and staring ahead in a shocked expression. The tongue had swollen up and forced the lips into a cross between a grin and a snarl. The detectives turned the body, patting the pockets, and Chumna pulled a wallet from one of them. I could see that it was full of paper money. He extracted an ID card and held it up to the face. The two exchanged knowing glances. One of them called out to me, "Do you know someone called Nic Stavriedies?"

That could be difficult to explain. I sort of did, but until I knew a bit more about the situation that I found myself in, I didn't feel happy admitting it. So I said nothing.

They both emerged from the bathroom. "Who did you say you were?" said the tall one.

"I didn't. I'm Miles Goram and I've only just got here."

He consulted his notebook, nodding.

"That's what it says here," he said, "but you haven't answered me, do you know him?"

"I know who he is, was, but I've never met him before, only talked to him, that's why I'm here."

"And why are you here?" This came from the short one, Chumna or whatever it was.

"I'm a writer, and I was supposed to be doing a piece about Nic Stavriedies and his hotel."

2

Chumna stood between me and the door; we looked at each other in awkward silence as Flanagan went into the corridor and made several calls on his phone. When he'd finished he came back: "The desk says that the room was booked from yesterday in your name," he said, "but you reckon you just got here. You mind explaining that."

That was the easy bit. "I should have been here yesterday, but there was a problem with the shuttle, magnetic storm or something, we had to delay landing." He made a note.

"I'm going to search the room," said Chumna, "do you want to open the safe?" I didn't think it was a question.

I activated the thumblock and opened the door. I took out my wallet, travel papers and my tablet computer and after giving them a quick look he bent down and shone his torch into the safe to see if there was anything else inside.

Chumna then moved across to the closet. He opened the door and reached in, moving the clothes around. "These all yours?" he asked.

"Yes," I replied, neglecting to tell him about the jacket. I had spotted something, and it had made me wonder.

There was a knock at the door, and soon the room was filled with medics and uniforms. I realised that sleep would have to wait for a while. I was jostled into a corner by the scrum. A photographer had appeared and was taking multiple pictures of everything that he could, and then he switched to video and went into the bathroom with its grisly contents. Somehow a gurney was manoeuvred into the bathroom and the body was lifted onto it by two paramedics. As it was wheeled out, a sheet covering the staring eyes, I saw that I was right: the trousers matched the jacket that was hanging up in the closet. I glanced at the detectives. Chumna had pulled back one curtain and was looking out of the window, and Flanagan hadn't searched the closet. It looked like I was the only one who had spotted it. My contact must have hung the jacket up before someone killed him.

With the departure of the body, the throng started to leave, until it was just me and the two detectives. I was feeling very tired now and wished that they all would go away. And I was still thirsty.

"Just so that you know," Flanagan said, looking at his colleague, "at this point you're not a suspect, but given the fact that you knew of the deceased, we will want to ask you some more questions. We'll be back to talk to you again in the morning."

I nodded. I had visions of paperwork holding me up here for days, particularly if they had researched me and got hold of my record. I could be here forever if they jumped to the wrong conclusion. And I was on a tight budget with no prospect of any more payment. Even though I cared about her, mentally I cursed Gaynor Rice and her 'could you just' request. "Oh please, Miles," she had said, "it's a nice easy job, you'll be in and out in a couple of days, and it's all expenses paid." I knew that she was only trying to help; we had been more than friends back when and she was the only one from my past who had stuck with me. But once you were heading down, it seemed like one bad thing followed another.

"Of course," said Chumna, "you can't stop here, you gotta change rooms – this is a crime scene. So pack up your stuff and go." My day wasn't getting any better and his attitude annoyed me.

"That's all very well," I said, "but where do I go?" I thought it was a reasonable question.

He looked exasperated. "It's not my problem..." he started, but got a look from his partner. "Oh hell," he muttered. "OK OK, I'll call the desk."

It wasn't that I minded changing rooms, in fact I was quite keen, but I wasn't in the mood to go finding my own bed for the night. Chumna made a call, while I grabbed all my gear. I was careful to hide the jacket as I bundled everything into my case. I was taken to an identical room along the corridor and the two detectives left.

I locked the door and put the chain on. No one was going to disturb my slumbers – I had no reason to get up anymore and I was going to have a lie-in. If the detectives wanted to talk to me, well they would just have to wait.

As I was putting my clothes into the closet, I felt a lump in the pocket of my newly acquired jacket. I rummaged around but it seemed to be inside the fabric, and I had to slit the lining to get it out. Suddenly sleep seemed less important than finding out if this could have been a reason for murder.

It was a drive-store, a small computer memory stick, and I took out my tablet and unrolled it. The holoscreen sprang to life and I paired it with the drive. There was only one file listed and I hit play. As it started I realised that I was looking at a news story from about two years ago. I recognised the story – it was me who had written it.

'BALCOM INDUSTRIAL HEIRESS MISSING, PRESUMED KIDNAPPED' was the strapline, and the video showed Layla Balcom in society news items, opening a Balcom Industrial factory, skiing on the Galthon Alps and generally having a good time, whilst my voice described her life and the events leading up to her disappearance.

A tall, strikingly pretty red-head with green eyes, she had been no stranger to the gossip columns, and stories of her love life alone had kept many a journalist, including me, employed. I had never met her, or even been anywhere near her, but that hadn't stopped me writing about her. I didn't make outrageous stuff up like some of them, but most of my articles, although true, were second-hand news. It had made me a good living, but that was all in my past.

As I remembered it, time had passed and the case had gone cold, all the sightings had proved false, but a few runaways who looked vaguely similar had received a shocking end to their adventures, and one government official had been caught disobeying his own laws, starting the chain of events that had led me to this hotel room.

Interest had eventually waned; the lack of new information and other, more exciting scandals had taken over, but I remembered one thing: a ransom had never been mentioned.

Next, there was a background piece on Layla's father, Igor Balcom. This one was by Gaynor Rice. Igor Balcom was more than just a businessman; he was the owner of factories and mines all across the sector. Balcom Industrial, under Igor's father and grandfather, had developed trans-light travel and had played a huge part in mankind's expansion across the galaxy. They owned space-liners and planetary hardware, and a whole lot more.

Igor had married late in life, and Layla was his only child. After his wife's death in an accident she became the sole heir to the company. Despite her busy social life, she had gone off and got herself qualified in Engineering and Planetary Surveying and was being groomed to take over Balcom Industrial. So she was not only smart and pretty; she was worth a lot. Then there was a brief interview with Igor, and his new PA, Donna Markes, where both pleaded tearfully for news of her, and offered an eye-wateringly large reward. Igor had aged about ten years in a few months and leaned on Donna as they spoke. The rumour was that they were an item, and the nastier gossip hinted at unladylike haste to become one of the Balcom family. But no one ever thought she would have gone as far as to kidnap Layla.

The news report ended, and a scanned document came up on the holoscreen. It was an entry form for Reevis, the sort you fill out on inbound flights, and the name on the top was Layla Balcom. It showed an official stamp at the bottom, just like the one I had got today on my own form, now residing in my wallet.

I paused the playback, I had forgotten about hotel reviews for a moment. Was this drive the real reason for me being here?

I wanted the past to stay in the past but I had to see the rest even though I thought I knew the story. I pressed play again and a voice which I recognised as Nic's spoke over the picture: "I know that's all familiar to you, Miles but that was just to refresh your memory. Now this is the interesting bit. Layla was reported missing two weeks before the entry date on this form, but no one else seems to have picked it up. I got this scan from a contact in Immigration Control, and although it appears to be genuine, there's no record in the log of its issue. More interesting than that, the hard copy has vanished. And there's more…"

I thought I heard a sound at my door and I stopped the playback. The holoscreen vanished. The noise came again; someone was rattling the door handle.

I crept to the door, turning off the lights, and peered through the spyhole. I could see the back of a uniformed police-man standing outside, hopping from foot to foot in a bored manner whilst scanning the hallway. It must have been him checking the door was locked. It looked like I had a guard; the detectives must have decided that I was the intended victim.

Suddenly feeling that I was out of my depth, I forgot the drive and laid out on the bed. I could feel sleep creeping up on me; the events of the last few hours were buzzing round in my head in a muddle. I would have to play the rest of the drive's contents tomorrow.

3

I awoke and for a second couldn't place myself; and then I remembered I was on Reevis, in the optimistically named Hotel Splendid. The mattress in this room had a hollow in the middle and I struggled to get out of it. I eventually rolled onto the floor with a thump. Getting up, I made my way to the bathroom and splashed some water on my face. I saw in the mirror that I was still wearing my clothes from yesterday. My watch said it was breakfast time – so much for the lie-in.

Looking in the mirror had brought it all back to me; I could almost see the body in the shower stall behind me, eyes staring. Nic was dead and I seemed to be at the centre of a mystery. I left the bathroom and moved stiffly to the window. Pulling back the thin curtains, I looked out on Reevis City.

My head felt like it was full of cotton wool as I tried to remember bits of information from the background tapes I had listened to on the journey.

Discovered over a century ago, in the rapid expansion of mankind that trans-light travel had started, Reevis was a place that we had looked at and swiftly passed by. If it hadn't been for the wealth of resources it had been found to contain when a spacecraft stopped and dropped a few probes, we would probably have never been back.

Long ago someone had described planets like this as Ribbon Worlds, referring to the thin ribbon of land that could just about support human life. And all that meant was that it wouldn't immediately kill you. In Reevis's case this was a strip about fifty miles across, circling the whole of its globe.

As the planet didn't rotate, one side was turned permanently towards the star, and so was too hot for life; metal flowed like water and volcanoes and earthquakes were constantly re-forming the land. In contrast, the other side, as it faced the nothingness of space, was too cold for any geological action and everything was frozen and desolate. The ribbon was a rocky bridge between the two.

There was no atmosphere to speak of so all of the human habitation was under a cluster of pressure domes. About the only thing going for it as a home for mankind was the gravity. This was similar to that on Earth, so moving around wasn't a problem.

There was no day or night on the ribbon, just a half-light that quickly brightened or faded depending on which way you travelled. The cluster itself was sheltered from direct sunlight, situated under the cliffs surrounding a large crater and close to the warm half. The crater was extensive and covered by ice on the cold side. Apart from the cluster there were a few other smaller domes, but only on the ribbon or on the cold side.

The domes in the main cluster were joined by tunnels and pressurised passageways. Energy here was plentiful, and man had found ways to use it. The ice on the cold side was made of methane, carbon dioxide and water, perfect for power generation and sustaining life. The hot side provided the means to melt and use it; lava flows had been tapped to provide a heat source to melt the ice and the whole set-up was a model of efficiency.

A lot of research and development went on both in the domes and outside using the vacuum conditions; it was considerably easier than doing it in orbit. All sorts of plants grew in the domes, providing food and decoration, and of course helping maintain the atmosphere. There was even a farm in its own dome, with fields of wheat and beans, cows and other animals. The cluster was like a self-sufficient island, on the edge of nowhere.

The population was increasing quickly, and as the industry developed and profits were made, more and more support was needed. There were upwards of twenty thousand people living on Reevis; it was getting positively crowded. And not all of them were workers; families had been brought in and a society was being built.

Looking out of my window, I could see the skin of the dome with its hexagonal panels, about half a mile away across the tops of the buildings. The lights reflecting off of the Plastoglass and metal frame gave the view a festive air, a bit like Christmas lights in a window.

Not that I was feeling particularly festive – the man I had come to see had been lying dead in my hotel room, and although I had been told that I was not a suspect, I still felt uncomfortable. And then there was the mysterious jacket, with its potentially explosive contents.

I wondered if there was anything else in the jacket and examined it carefully under the desk light. There was a business card in the top pocket, for something called Al's Tours; it advertised trips to 'A Land of Flames and Frigo.' I smiled at the mangling of language – so much for amalgamation. Apart from that there was nothing in the jacket or its lining that I could find. I hung it back up in the closet, behind my clothes.

I had a shave and a shower, with a blast of cold water at the end to wake me up. I was just pulling fresh clothes on and deciding whether to face breakfast or view the rest of the stuff on the drive first when the internal phone rang. I picked it up and before I could say anything, Detective Flanagan's voice informed me that he was just starting breakfast downstairs and would like to ask me some questions.

I sighed. It had to be done I guess and it was probably better done here over food than in the station. I was faintly relieved that it was him and not Chumna, who had seemed less friendly. Or perhaps that was just the way they worked and it was Flanagan's turn to be good cop today.

"OK, I'll be down," I said and put the drive in my pocket. I put my tablet and papers in the safe, locking it with my thumbprint, and opened the door. The policeman was still on guard and he avoided eye contact as I came out of the room and locked up. I thought it was the same one but couldn't be sure. I'd only seen the back of his neck through the spyhole. His uniform cap was pulled down over his eyes, the brim hiding his face in shadow.

He ignored my "Good morning" and turned his face away from me. He probably thought I was guilty of something. I caught a strong whiff of his aftershave; maybe I'd spoilt his plans for last night. Well this place had certainly spoilt mine, so we were even. As I passed, I noticed that his badge said 'LEVSON, REEVIS CITY POLICE'. I shrugged and made my way to the lift.

It was still out of action, so I used the stairs again.

There was no one at the desk as I crossed the lobby towards the restaurant. The corridor was the same multi-coloured fibreboard as the rooms, with the same signs of wear and tired finish. Some of the strip lights were out and one flashed and buzzed as I walked under it. Looking up I could see dead flies trapped in the shade. I realised that I was hungry as I caught a whiff of fried food and fresh coffee.

The restaurant was a brightly lit space with a bar in one corner, shuttered up and closed at this time of day. I spotted Flanagan at the same time as he saw me; he was already eating his breakfast and waved me over.

His plate of eggs and meats looked appetising and when the waitress eventually wandered across, I ordered the same, as she slopped coffee into my cup with bored indifference. The room was more like a factory canteen than a hotel restaurant, all plastic tables and harsh lights. There were a few people eating, but the place was not more than a quarter full. They were all working men, dressed in overalls and intent on the food; there were no tourists visible here.

"Good morning, you sleep OK?" asked Flanagan. "It must have been a shock to you."

"You can say that again," I replied. "Like I said, I was supposed to be reviewing a hotel, now I'll have to warn people to check for a body in the bathroom." He smiled at that. "And was it your idea to put a guard outside my door overnight?" I asked.

He looked up. "No," he replied, with a puzzled expression, "that must have been Chummie." I could see the wheels turning in his head. He changed the subject: "You said you were supposed to meet him, this corpse. Tell me about it."

I took a mouthful of coffee and a deep breath, and gave him the story.

"I work freelance these days, but mainly for the flash-mag *Getaway*," I told him. "The editor, Gaynor Rice, asked me if I could come out here and do a piece on Nic Stavriedies – all their regulars were busy."

"And was that unusual?" His eyes narrowed.

I thought about saying, 'No, she felt sorry for me because I'm nearly broke.' The truth was that I was surviving on her kindness and the memory of the thing that we used to have. Instead I said, "Not at all, it's how I work; I get the same sort of request from lots of mags." I thought to myself, 'you wish' but tried to keep the successful journalist act up. "Anyway Gaynor was paying so I wasn't going to argue. It was run-of-the-mill stuff. I did a bit of research before I left; I found that Nic has, or should I say had, a new hotel on Reevis and was trying to advertise this place as the ultimate holiday destination. I guess he hoped Gaynor could get him a good write-up and boost his visitor numbers."

Flanagan nodded around his breakfast, talking as he chewed: "If you've researched him then you'll know all about the problems that Nic was having."

This was news to me. Gaynor had never mentioned problems, and he had kept it off the search engines, apart from the usual start-up niggles that every new venture experiences. I reckoned that that was part of the reason for my coming, to show that the teething troubles were over and the place was ready.

"Nothing more specific than a few minor glitches," I answered, "but I figured that the upmarket hotel trade can't be easy here. I mean, this isn't exactly a pleasure planet, is it? The cost of set-up means you need a big return, or customers with deep pockets." I almost added, 'Mind you, if this place is the competition, then he should do well,' but thought better of it.

He shook his head. "I didn't mean that. There was opposition from the mining and tech companies – they didn't want a tourist hotel at all, or loads of extra people around." He took a deep breath. "Maybe I shouldn't be telling you, and if you put any of this in your article I will be in deep trouble, but Nic had made lots of enemies." That got my attention.

"OK," I nodded, "off the record then, just background."

He continued, looking relieved, "The research companies reckoned some of his ideas were a security risk; they just don't like the idea of tourists wandering around. The popular expression is 'off-worlders'. They say that they're concerned about industrial espionage, making it too easy to get on and off world, that sort of thing. That was one of the reasons Reevis started up – it was easy to keep secure. Nic was threatened, but we could never pin down by whom, and when that failed to put him off, the companies lobbied the Mayor."

I nodded. "Let me guess, the Mayor sided with the big business?"

He looked uncomfortable. "Well, let's just say that the Mayor knew where her power-base lay."

That stopped me for a moment. I don't know why but I had expected the Mayor of Reevis to be a man. Flanagan noticed my look. "Before that I would never have said she was a figurehead, or a soft touch. She's an ex-test pilot and pretty tough. But clearly she had been persuaded. In the end she couldn't find a legitimate way to stop him altogether, but she could make it difficult for him. First she managed to stop him building under this roof. For a time it looked like he was going to have to finance his own dome, away from the cluster."

I could tell that to build a dome would have needed serious money, so either Nic was very rich, or he had backers who were. I thought of what I had seen so far on the drive – maybe he had been blackmailing someone about Layla to finance his business, and it had got out of hand. Stranger things had happened.

This was all interesting stuff, and I could see an angle for my piece to the mag: 'The Unwanted Tourists' or something along those lines. Clearly there was still a story here; even without Nic, his hotel would still be running, and staff would still be employed. I mentally put the Mayor on my list of people to see, along with this Al.

Flanagan was still talking, but I was thinking about the cost of building your own dome and wasn't really listening when something he said made me snap back to the present. "The main opponents were Balcom Industrial. They're the biggest players here; perhaps you need to speak to them."

To say that was a surprise would be an understatement, and I nearly told him what I had seen last night; with that information it made things a whole lot more interesting. But

I thought better of it. Instead I added Balcom to my list.

My food arrived, and I had a coffee refill. As I tucked in Flanagan watched me, which I found slightly unnerving; perhaps it was meant to be. I hadn't eaten since yesterday afternoon, just before landing, so I was ravenous.

"What do you think?" He waved his fork at my plate. "It's real food; all locally grown, no artificial proteins."

"It's pretty good stuff," I mumbled through half-chewed food, and it was. There was no trace of the slight tang that you sometimes get from hydroponically grown plants or in meat from animals fed on them. And it had a flavour you miss after freeze-dried or vac-packed rations.

"That was another of Nic's ideas," Flanagan went on, "make his place a food lovers' paradise. In the end he teamed up with a man called Al Nichols – he's a local businessman and amongst other things, fronts the farm co-operative that produced your breakfast."

That would be Al's tours, I thought to myself, but I didn't mention the card I had found.

"Al's another one that the big boys don't like too much," continued Flanagan. "They can't control him, but they need him, and he and Nic got on well so were natural partners. Between them they talked the farmers into giving Nic space for his hotel in their dome, and in the end there was nothing that the Mayor or anyone else could do about it."

He stopped there and resumed his watching routine as I ate the rest of my food. I had imagined Reevis to be a quiet place. How wrong could I be?

When I had finished eating Flanagan spoke again: "It's been bothering me, I recognised your name but couldn't place you." Here it comes, I thought. "Yes," he continued, "weren't you the journalist who…"

I stopped him there; I didn't want to discuss my past, especially with a policeman who may not be too sympathetic.

"That's me," I sighed, "but I don't like to be reminded, if that's OK with you."

He shrugged. "Alright, it had been bothering me, that's all. Come on then," he said, "I think I ought to go and meet this guard of yours." Together we went back up the stairs to my room. We didn't even bother trying the lift.

The guard was gone, and my door was open.

Flanagan drew his pistol and stepped inside, and as he didn't tell me otherwise I followed him. The room had been trashed, and the safe door was open. With a sinking feeling I looked inside; my tablet and papers were still there as was my wallet. I looked inside it, and my meagre supply of cash and my cards were present, which surprised me. I shut the safe door and surveyed the wreckage. The closet was open, doors on the floor, and my clothes were in a pile on the bed. It didn't take long to see that the jacket wasn't there. Of course I had the drive in my pocket, so in that respect they hadn't found what they were looking for. But Flanagan didn't know anything about that.

"What's missing?" he asked me.

"Nothing, as far as I can see," I replied carefully, "and they opened the safe, but they left all my papers and my money. Where was your guard then?"

"I didn't know about a guard, that was why I came up here."

We heard running on the stairs and Chumna burst into the room; the gun in his hand was shaking and he was short of breath, sweat running down his face. "There you are," he panted, and then he caught sight of Flanagan. "Hey, Barry," he gasped, "what are you...doing here?"

"What's going on, Chummie?" asked Flanagan. "Why didn't you tell me you put a guard on, and where is he?"

Chumna gasped out his answers: "I put...him on... thought they might be back...maybe Nic wasn't the real target...Sergeant Bates...said he went to the lavatory... when he returned there...were two of them in...the room." He paused, chest heaving. "One was in the...bathroom... hit him and they ran...when Bates got up he chased them, and called me...but they split up and we lost them." He put his hands on his knees and gulped air. "Anything missing?"

"You must have disturbed them in time," I said, "nothing's been taken; but does this mean I'm not safe here? After what I've heard this morning, I'm pretty concerned."

Flanagan looked annoyed, as if I shouldn't have said that. "I don't know; we don't get many murders here, or many travel writers come to that. You seem to have brought nothing but trouble with you."

My thoughts were that there was enough trouble here already, just bubbling under the surface; perhaps I was the catalyst that would bring it all into the open. And who was Bates? The badge had said Levson.

Flanagan looked across at his partner, who was still wheezing. He thought for a minute and turned back to me. "I think we'd better keep an eye on you, Mr Miles Goram."

4

I could understand their suspicion, but I wasn't letting on any more than I had to until I knew the situation better. And the policeman's name was nagging at my mind. He had said Bates but the badge had read Levson. When Chumna had stopped wheezing he called for a forensics team to come and search the room for evidence.

I was worried irrespective of the name, and there was probably a simple explanation for that; the fact that they had waited till the police guard had left meant they had probably been watching the door. That spoke of an organisation. I guessed that whoever they were, they were after the drive and having seen it the reason was obvious. But I wanted to think before I rushed off and started using the information so I didn't mention it. Perhaps now that they had the empty jacket they might leave me alone and look somewhere else. I was worried about where I was going to stay so I persuaded the detectives to speak to the hotel management, who I thought would probably refuse me another room.

Their resigned acceptance of another crime made me think that they were used to this sort of thing; maybe with all the casual workers they got, they were. Whatever the reason, I got my third room, still the same as the other two, and went through the familiar routine of unpacking again.

I had already decided that I wasn't going to stop here any longer than I had to; maybe after I had met this man Al, I could get a room at Nic's hotel. I hadn't wanted to stop there initially, at least until I had done some incognito research, in case it prejudiced the service for a better review. But I was only getting a fixed fee for the job, so I didn't want to take any longer than I had to before I sent off my article. Then if I had any money left, I would be free to relax and have a bit of a break before I headed off back to civilisation.

Deciding on my plan for the day, I would have a look around the dome, copy Nic's drive and post it off world, maybe get a sense of the locals' feelings about the hotel and see some of the people on my list. I put smart clothes on – if I might be seeing the Mayor I didn't want to look too scruffy.

On my way out, I paused at the desk. The clerk was reading a holomag, the page shimmering in mid-air in front of his face. It wasn't one of Gaynor's as far as I could tell. I could see his expression change as he saw me through the words; they flicked off as he shut the power to his tablet.

"Well it's Mr-give-me-another-room-Goram," he said with a grin. "What can we do for you? I think we still have some on the fifth floor that you haven't tried yet."

"Hey, don't look at me," I replied, "I'm fed up with unpacking. Anyway they're all the same."

"It's true," he answered, "but you still have a way to go to keep up with some of our regulars, although a body and a theft in twelve hours puts you pretty high up the list."

I played along, "At least some of the furniture is still intact."

"That's a different way of doing things," he agreed. "We're used to the police, with our varied clientele, and even a bit of breakage, but normally detectives don't come and vouch for the guests, they just take them away." He became serious. "You're not going out dressed like that are you?"

I looked down at my trousers; I was decent. "What do you mean?" I asked.

"Well, you scream off-worlder, and they're not the most popular of folk around here."

"Why's that then?" I hadn't expected to hear it expressed

so openly; maybe it tied in with what Flanagan had said about the tech companies not wanting tourists.

"There's a lot of paranoia about security, the companies don't want random bodies lurking about." He looked nervous. "That's their words. I'm all for new faces, a bit of variety."

"Surely you've already got non-essentials here, wives and kids, that sort of thing."

"Yes and some of the old-timers don't think it's a good place for them either. Look, I think you need all sorts to make a colony, and the secure stuff isn't in this dome anyway, I'm just telling you how it is. If I were you, I'd stay away from dark alleys." He turned his magazine back on with a shrug.

That gave me a bit to think about as I left the hotel and walked across the street. I had seen a line of shops on my way in yesterday and where better to get a handle on the mood in a settlement than at a coffee shop. And I needed a blank drive to copy the one I had found. There were quite a few people about, some in overalls and working gear, but there were more than a few who were clearly not working, either enjoying time off, or maybe just didn't work.

I could see straight away what the desk clerk had meant; everyone's clothing was bland and functional compared to my city attire and I stood out. People stared at me and I wondered why there was such a dislike of anyone who was not seen as local. After all, no one here was really local, some of them had just been here longer than others.

I felt their eyes boring into me, but perhaps I was just reacting to the things I had heard. Surely it couldn't be that unfriendly. I tried saying good morning to the people that passed, but hardly anyone answered me, and some even turned away from me as I approached.

It probably didn't help that I wasn't really happy about being here under the dome. It made me feel uneasy that I was dependant for my survival on a couple of layers of

Plastoglass and an automated power station. I knew that I was not alone in that; a large number of people were phobic to this way of life, despite the fact that only a few domes had ever had problems. When they did, of course, the results tended to be spectacular.

My fears were based on the well-known fact that no dome is ever completely airtight; there has to be an atmosphere plant producing positive pressure all the time as air seeps out through the interface between the dome and the bedrock. The positive pressure also helps relieve the strain on the dome itself, supporting some of the weight of the frame and panels, allowing for bigger structures. Of course there was also leakage between the panels and the frame no matter how well they had been sealed.

Once again I was amazed at the amount of information I had remembered from the tapes on the liner. I had listened to them a couple of times, and set them to play subliminally while I slept, and quite a bit of it had stuck. Some of it had even helped; the rest had just terrified me.

I had learnt that on Reevis the atmosphere was manufactured by melting ice from the cold side of the planet, using a diverted lava flow from the hot side. The main products from this melt were water, methane and carbon dioxide. The water was split by electrolysis, using electricity generated from steam turbines, old technology in this fusion age but still dependable and efficient. Oxygen was then available for pressurising the domes.

The methane and hydrogen were stored for fuel and the carbon dioxide was added back into the atmosphere to aid photosynthesis in the domes. The atmosphere was then bulked out with nitrogen obtained from mining the nitrate deposits which had been found on the cold side.

Lost in my thoughts, I had got to the edge of the roadway, marked with a line of white stones. Automatically

I looked left and, seeing no traffic, stepped into the road. An open-topped vehicle coming from the other way just missed me, and I received a barrage of honking and shouting from the driver as I jumped back. The only word I heard clearly was 'off-worlder'.

This was one of the worlds where they drove on the left then. I had been so tired last night that I hadn't noticed. After years of arguing, planets were still split into left and right-handed drivers. Strangely on water and in space everyone everywhere kept to the right.

I had attracted a small crowd who tutted and shook their heads at my stupidity. Mustering my dignity I looked again, both ways this time, and when it was safe, crossed the road.

I saw several types of vehicles using the roads; most were open-topped utility vehicles with or without flat beds and there were some enclosed vehicles as well. They all kicked up grey dust, which blew sideways in a gentle breeze. The streets were unpaved, just strips of the bedrock that had been compacted and levelled.

The dark grey rock was randomly scattered with tufts of coloured moss, some of them quite substantial. It never ceased to amaze me, nature's ability to thrive, given the chance. The rock was supposed to be inert, but the spores had somehow managed to grow on it. The rosy half-light through the dome was shot with bursts of brighter red, a bit like the aurora only twice as beautiful. It silhouetted the tall cliffs behind us. No one else seemed to notice it.

As I walked on I came to a green space, framed with foliage. I'm no expert but amongst the random mixture I recognised oaks and pines mixed with rhododendrons and hydrangea. Under them the soil was covered with a mixture of lawns and bedding plants, bright colours from pansies and geraniums.

It looked like the whole thing had been planted in a large

container, let into a hole dug in the rock. And I mean large – this one was at least two hundred metres long and maybe fifty wide, in an 'S' shape bisecting the town. It showed commitment, a determination to make this place home. The plants framed a small stream fringed with rocks, dragonflies buzzed over the clear water. The hum of the pump was barely noticeable. The leaves were spotted with what looked like raindrops and the air smelt damp. It added a homely touch to the alien landscape, and I daresay helped the oxygen cycle as well. Small children ran on the grass chasing each other between the trees whilst parents sat on benches or blankets on the grass.

There was a whoosh of wings and a flock of pigeons passed overhead. I looked up at them and saw more on the frames of the dome. I hadn't expected that, but I guess they were part of the food chain. There would probably be all sorts of animal life to balance the ecology – there was no doubt that this place was here to stay.

Less inspiring was the graffiti that I could see scrawled on the sides of the buildings. 'Off-Worlders go home' and 'No more useless mouths' were the dominant sentiments, visible from yards away, formed with angry strokes of black paint. Most of the buildings were made of plastic composite panels; a lot of them showed multi-coloured patches where previous slogans had been painted over. The graffiti made me feel uncomfortable, standing there as I was in my off-world clothes.

5

I had reached the line of shops without incurring anyone else's wrath and went into the general store. It was one of those places that you find on any world that sells just about everything under one roof. This one had goods stacked on and hanging from every available place, so much so that I could hardly make out the man stood behind the counter. I wished him good morning and he gave me the look that he probably reserved for child murderers. I realised that I was starting to feel depressed with the place; whatever Nic's hotel was like it didn't feel like the sort of place I would want to come for a holiday.

The store was the usual Aladdin's cave of random stuff. A lot of it seemed designed to work in vacuum while you were wearing a pressure-suit, a line of which were hung up on a rail like a row of beef carcasses in a freezer. Video screens showed adverts for vehicles of all sorts, and there were stacks of prospecting gear, with warning signs around the sharper or more destructive items. A big red poster advised that anyone under twenty-one could not buy explosives.

All in all there was more than enough equipment here to run a colony. I moved through an archway to a second large room. This one had more creature comforts: a shelf of up-to-date movies, computer games, clothing and food. There was a distinction between the locally produced supplies, called 'dome-made', and the imports. Naturally the imports were ten times the price of the local stuff. Surprisingly, the range of local produce was extensive, and contained a lot of luxury items: wine, oysters, chocolate and tobacco. There was a fresh food counter as well, with vegetables, meat and a dairy section. The farm must be some place; I was looking forward to seeing it.

A group of people were sat in the corner talking, and I couldn't help but overhear them as I searched for the things I wanted. Most places have such a group, the ones that are always writing letters to the council, the noisy ones with opinions, and these were no exception. They were all older people, four men and a woman, holding cups of coffee and glaring at the world in general.

The general argument seemed to be that Reevis was getting too big, and the people were becoming soft, not real pioneers like them. Especial venom was reserved for computer games and just about any sort of creature comfort. They spotted me looking around and glared some more; there was a lot of muttering that I couldn't hear and then they shut up. I moved away, and as if I had flicked a switch their conversation restarted.

This time the topic was the farming dome. They complained that the food had been better and cheaper when Balcom ran the farm, and how the extra people living on Reevis were straining the farm's ability to feed everyone. According to them, the place was finished unless major investment was made, and no one was apparently willing to do that. If you had listened to them any longer, you would have thought that the colony was on its knees, and they would all be eating the pigeons soon.

This sounded strange to me, as the tapes had suggested that as Reevis made so much money for Balcom, and hence tax for the Federation, its survival was practically guaranteed. I moved away, having spotted the computer supplies on a rack near the front window, making a mental note to ask Flanagan or Al about it.

Of course I found everything I needed. I bought a pack of blank drive-stores identical to the one I had found in

Nic's jacket, together with a prepaid envelope, good for off-world postage and a few other bits and pieces, creature comforts that my friends sitting in the back would have hated. My credit card went through without a hitch, so Gaynor's advance must have hit my account on the way out here, just like she had said it would. I missed her and debated calling her later.

I left the store intending to go into the coffee shop next door. I wanted to copy Nic's drive onto my new one and get it off world and safe as quickly as I could. Then I heard the shop door open and close behind me. Turning, I saw that one of the group that I had been eavesdropping on had followed me out and decided to try and get a bit more out of him if I could.

"Excuse me, sir," I shouted, trying to be polite, respectable and friendly all in one go.

He gave me a suspicious glance. "Yes, Mr Off-Worlder," was his sarcastic reply, "what do you want to know?"

"I couldn't help overhearing your discussion in the store," I started and his eyes narrowed.

"We thought you were paying attention," there was a hint of a smile on his face, "but then we figured that you must have been one of our lovely Mayor's secret police."

"Well I can assure you that I'm not." Why did this place need secret police? Flanagan had said it was quiet. "I've just arrived and I want to know a bit about the place."

He gave me a suspicious look. "That's what you say, but I'm not falling for it, not after what happened to Harry." He looked up and down the road, and seeing us alone he continued, "If you're thinking of staying on Reevis, my advice is don't. That's all I'm saying, if you want any more you'd better ask your boss." Seeing my puzzled look he added, "You know, the Mayor...or Balcom – after all, it's the same thing around here." He turned and walked away.

Stranger and stranger, I thought as I walked across to the coffee shop and went through the swing doors.

The place was modelled on a historic ideal of the small-town diner, a long counter with stools and the cook behind it on one side with booths on the opposite side. There was lots of gingham in bright reds and blues, it adorned just about everything. After the grey outside it almost made my eyes hurt. The seats were all red leather with white-topped tables and the chrome work gleamed.

The place was busy. There were groups of women sipping coffee and chatting, teenagers swinging on the stools, and a bunch of miners sitting in the corner, eating huge plates of food and laughing loudly. Ceiling fans swung lazily as I slipped into the only empty booth and sat, laying my purchases out on the table in front of me.

"You vacationing, or on business?" asked the waitress as she poured my coffee. Tall, blond and far too young for me, her voice had a bubbly, friendly quality, and I felt better for hearing it. She had a tight red gingham uniform with 'Dome Diner' embroidered on it. "Your clothes give you away as an off-worlder, no offence, and anyway I've not seen you around before." Her name badge said Macie. It suited her.

"None taken," I answered. "I'm working, but I only got here yesterday and I'm still getting used to the place." I thought that the body in the bathroom story would not be a good conversation piece so I kept it to myself.

"Oh right," she replied, still smiling, "who did you upset to end up here? Well if there's anything you want to know, just ask." I was surprised after the surly attitudes so far to be treated like a normal person. I assumed that her remark about upsetting people was just a bit of friendly banter, but it added to my overall impression of the place. I could think of about a hundred questions, but started with the last thing I had noticed.

"OK, well if we're in a sealed pressure dome, where does the breeze and the rain come from?"

"Good question." She sounded impressed. "Well it's all—"

The door crashed open and a large man in stained miners overalls and a yellow jacket came in just as she was about to tell me. All conversation ceased as his piggy eyes swivelled around the room, taking in all the occupants in an instant. He had a shaved head, with a red weal around it from a safety helmet, and heavy gloves tucked into his belt. His gaze stopped as it settled on me. "Macie," he growled, "When you're done talking to off-worlders, there's a working man," and he said that a little louder, "who needs service." And he turned and walked to his mates in the corner. They greeted him with raised voices and laughter, as the volume came back up.

She rolled her eyes. "That's Harris Morgan. He's the most important man on Reevis," she grinned, "in his head. I'll tell you later." She wandered off towards him smiling, the coffee pot swinging in her hand. "Hi, Harris, what can I get you?"

Sipping my coffee, which was strong with a deep bittersweet tang, I paired Nic's drive with my new one and copied the contents across. Then I put the copied drive in the envelope and sealed the flap. Taking out my stylus, I addressed it to myself, care of Gaynor Rice at the magazine offices on Centra, ready to drop it into the post. Gaynor would look after it for me till I could pick it up; she might even resist the temptation to look at it. Once it was in the post, it would be safe.

The miner she had called Harris was sat with the others in the corner and was watching me. Initially I hadn't noticed, as I was intent on my task. Now I felt his gaze on me. At first I tried to avoid it, and then I thought, why? I stared right back. He said something to his mates, which got them all laughing, and then he lumbered to his feet and came over to me.

"Anyone ever told you it's rude to stare?" He planted

his fists, about the size of two good bunches of bananas, on the table, the force spilling my coffee. People looked up at the noise and the place went quiet again.

"I didn't start it," I replied calmly. "You've been staring at me since you got here."

"Be careful, lad," he spoke slowly, "we don't like strangers here, or tourists, lots of dangerous things around for off-worlders, and it's very easy to die here."

"Hey, Harris," the waitress had come back over, with that sixth sense for trouble that they all possess, "gentleman's just arrived – for all you know he could be your new boss. Let him be."

He stalked back to his seat, muttering about off-worlders and I saw the back of his overalls. He had taken the jacket off, revealing a drawing of a planet split in two by a yellow lightning bolt; underneath it said BALCOM.

I decided it would be wise to drink up and leave, so I went to the desk and paid for my coffee. I asked Macie where the post office was and she gave me directions. "Take no notice of Harris," she said, "he's been here so long, he thinks it's his planet." She lowered her voice, "Far as I care he can have it, I'm off just as soon as I can get the fare."

I wandered along the street and found the post office. Dropping the envelope into the box made me feel a lot better; at least Nic's story would get out and maybe I could follow it up a bit whilst I was here. As I turned away from the box, out of the corner of my eye I saw a figure duck back into an alleyway. I must be getting paranoid because as I looked again a small boy appeared, kicking a ball.

I had a choice, see the Mayor or visit Nic's hotel. I didn't know where the hotel was, but City Hall was right in front of me, so that seemed as good a place as any to start. As I crossed the street, remembering to look the right way this time, I wondered at the reception I would get and what I might have to say to get an audience. There was a solitary policeman on duty outside the door; he looked me up and down and nodded to me as he let me pass.

For a relatively new world, on the inside it was a shabby place, all faded rugs scattered over dirty tiles and tired-looking furniture. There were a couple of pictures on the walls of the construction of the dome and groups of suited workers dwarfed by machinery and metal. I walked up to the desk and found it manned by an older woman with cropped hair. She eyed me suspiciously. "I'm looking for a couple of minutes with the Mayor," I said.

Her lips turned down. "That won't be possible, Mr…?"

"Miles Goram," I answered her, giving my best smile.

"Well, Mr Goram," she replied with the power of a gate-keeper, "our Mayor is a very busy person; perhaps you could tell me what it's all about?"

"A private matter," I answered her.

"I see." She looked me straight in the eye, her thirst for gossip unquenched. "Well it might be possible…" She rifled through screens on her computer. "How about ten days from now, at six pm?"

It was obvious that unless she got some juicy details, I was kicking my heels.

"Okay," I said and turned to leave. "Oh, can you tell the Mayor I called, and can you also tell her that it's about Nic Stavriedies, and I'll be back in an hour." As I approached the door, the entrance swung open and Harris Morgan came in. He looked me straight in the eye but said nothing and I kept on walking.

To pass the hour, I took a wander around the town, deciding to find out how to get to the hotel in the farming dome. The buildings were a collection of prefabricated structures, all in different styles laid out along roadways lined with potted trees and bushes. Some were terraced in long rows whilst others had their own plot of land around them on all sides. The uses seemed to be a mixture of residential and business, all lumped together as if they had grown that way.

It didn't take me long to start feeling like I was being followed. I could sense a presence behind me. Although every time I looked around there were never the same people twice, I was still sure.

The graffiti was repeated at intervals, and there were more signs that other slogans had been painted and covered. It certainly wasn't a welcoming place. There was a lot of litter and wild vegetation in the alleys between a lot of the buildings, and pigeon droppings stained a lot of the surfaces. There were weeds surviving on the rubbish that had been thrown away and I was reminded of the desk clerk's warning. But I could also see that there was plenty of space for expansion in this dome. The people that I saw hurried about and were oblivious to my greetings.

I was wandering around when I saw Macie, the girl from the diner. She saw me at the same time and came over. "Hi there," she greeted me, "you seeing the sights?" She waved her arm around at the covered graffiti. "Friendly bunch aren't they, but I guess you've found that out already."

"I was just thinking, if I was living in a bubble on a world like this, I think I would be more concerned with staying alive than with how long my neighbour had been here, or what they did."

"Good point," she agreed, nodding her head, the curls moving around like a wave breaking, "but it's safer now than it used to be, and people get lazy."

"How do you mean?"

"Well, now that there are people here who don't actually have a function, you know like dome techs or atmosphere controllers, well with nothing to do they have time on their hands. And the ones working hard resent that."

She was pretty perceptive; maybe it came from seeing all sorts in the diner. I put my journalist's hat on. "So if you're useful you're OK?" She nodded. "What's your story then?"

"My parents were early settlers. Dad is a process manager at the power plant and Mother works on the farm. I'm qualified in plant genetics and terraforming, I'm just working at the diner to pay off my study debts, while I try and find a job somewhere, hopefully not here."

We had strolled along together, in a bit of a circle as it happened, because I saw we were back by City Hall. My hour was nearly up; it was time to face the Mayor.

"Good luck with that," I said, "and thanks for the background. You said in the diner you couldn't wait to get away."

She grinned. "You ask too many questions. Well let's just say I want to be free." She paused for a moment, then continued; "Oh yes, the rain is produced by sprinklers on the framework and the breeze is the only way of making sure we stay alive. My dad says that there are so many leaks in the dome that the power plant is working flat out producing atmosphere to keep positive pressure. The breeze is the atmosphere escaping through the holes." And with that she turned to go. "One more thing," she said with a carefree shrug, "they have to be careful to keep the atmospheric pressure just about right – too low and the dome would collapse under its own weight." She paused for effect. "Of course if it gets too high it would blow the roof off!"

Pigeons flocked overhead and I thought that I saw a hawk of some sort chasing them.

I returned to the Mayor's office, the policeman nodded again and I took a seat in the waiting room. The chair was threadbare and stuffing was escaping in places.

There was a different receptionist, just as severe looking as the last one – perhaps they were sisters. She eyed me curiously. "You're new here," she said. "Your clothes are too clean, and I don't recognise you. Do you have an appointment?"

"I would like to see the Mayor," I repeated my request and walked up to the desk to show her my ID card. She held it as though it might contaminate her.

"I thought so, off-worlder… Hmm, a journalist, we don't get many of them round here. What are you writing about?"

I was just considering what to tell her – a hotel review, a dead businessman or a missing girl; and what was all the off-worlder stuff, weren't we all citizens? – when there was a shove in my back. I turned – it was my friend from the diner. He faced me, eyes blazing. "You again, and a bloody newspaperman! There's nothing to see or write about here, it's all confidential, you'd be better off getting out while you still can." His face was red in his rage and his fists twitched in anticipation of further explaining.

I didn't like his attitude, and his size made me a fool to try it, but by now I was fed up with the whole planet, so I shoved him in the chest, as hard as I could. He didn't move; it was about the same as pushing a rock.

"Don't tell me where I can be," I said forcefully. "I'm invited, unlike your comments. It makes me wonder, you seem to be hiding something." I saw his expression change. "Seems to me you protest too much, might make a man like me suspicious." He was shocked; I expect he wasn't used to being answered back and I thought that maybe I had found a sensitive spot.

Just then, a tall, elegant, dark-haired woman came out of an office behind him and walked toward us. She was dressed for the city in a white blouse and fitted skirt, with black-stockinged legs and heels that clicked on the tiled floor. "Harris," she said in a voice that radiated command, "what are you doing?"

"This journalist has been poking about, asking questions in the diner, and now he's here. I don't like it."

"It's not your concern, leave it to me." She held out her hand, "I'm Liberty Friedrich, the Mayor, what do you want?" Her grip was firm and her blue eyes looked straight at me.

"A bit of a private chat," I looked at Harris, "would be nice."

"OK," she said, "I've got five minutes spare, come into my office. Harris, get back to the plant, I'll call you later." He muttered something about watching me and stalked off. The receptionist was pretending not to notice but I reckoned she thought that she had some good gossip to trade.

6

The Mayor led me into her office and I was shocked at its simplicity; it was a bit better than my hotel room in terms of décor, but still more functional than most taxpayer-funded offices. There were large maps on the walls, showing the layout of the cluster, and a really big photograph of the crater in which we sat covered one wall. It showed our insignificance in the scale of the planet, and also showed the line of lava, lapping at the outer edge of the crater rim. There were several filing cabinets and a large table with lots of uncomfortable-looking chairs in addition to her desk.

She waved me to sit and went behind her large, overflowing desk. "You've met Harris Morgan before, I take it." She opened a drawer and passed me a bottle of ice-cold water; taking one for herself she opened it with a hiss.

"We've had words," I replied, toasting her with the bottle. The water tasted fresh, was slightly bubbly and had a faint tang of something pleasant. "That's good," I said.

"It's a by-product from the power plant, genuine Reevis water with no treatment." She put her bottle down and leant forwards. "So, Mr Goram, what can I do for you?"

"Do you know why I'm here? It will save a lot of explanation."

"I know that Nic wanted you to validate his ideas, and I know that he's dead. So I guess that means that you'll be off on the next liner."

This was a thread running through all my dealings so far and it seemed to me that my life would be considerably enhanced by leaving, but I had been given a job to do and my stubborn streak was coming through.

"Is his hotel still open?" I asked her. "Because if it is, I've still got a job to do. And I must admit I'm puzzled."

"Why is that then?"

"Well, I would have thought that a new source of income would be welcomed. After the Hotel Splendid, anywhere would be competition, yet everyone wants me gone."

She looked straight through me. "You have to understand," she said slowly, "this place is not a tourist haunt; it can be dangerous, and to be frank we have better things to do than keep an eye on people whose sole aim is wandering around trying to die. And believe me, it's very easy to die here. We probably lose a dozen or so every month and they are experienced men. Not only that but there is a lot of sensitive work going on, things that companies have spent a lot on, and the thought of losing commercial secrets gives them problems. They don't like the idea of uncontrolled tourism – there's too much chance for industrial espionage."

"But you have people here who aren't connected with the research," I answered.

"Yes we do," she conceded, "but they're all either the families of workers, or providing some other benefit to the community. They stay on Reevis, know the rules and don't go wandering around where they shouldn't be, taking pictures of everything." She paused for breath; her cheeks were flushed and I could tell that she was getting angry. "Now Nic, rest him," she continued, "made some friends in the farm and in the end we couldn't stop him building, but it doesn't mean we have to like it. So go and have a look if you feel that you must, but don't expect to do any good with your article, because, in the end, the people in charge here don't want what he has on offer. Now I'm very busy – shut the door on your way out."

I remembered what the old man had said to me outside

47

the hardware store. "Is that the Balcom line, or the politically independent Mayor's line?" I asked and she exploded.

"You'd better be really careful in what you say – I know all about you and your little difference of opinion with the delegate from Dalyster. Nic Stavriedies was an agitator and a troublemaker and he was only happy when he was stirring things up."

Now it was my turn to get angry. She had touched a nerve and was showing that she knew all about me. It suddenly made me wonder just how much of a coincidence this job really was. I pushed the chair back and jumped to my feet. "If you'd have done your homework a bit better, you would know that I was proved right and in the end I was absolved. And why shouldn't all your little secrets be exposed, just like the delegate's were? It keeps you honest and accountable."

"Yes," she was shouting now, "and your profession and your history have coloured your judgement; you see conspiracy everywhere. It's classic behaviour and it's wrong. The people don't need to know everything, only what's good for them."

She had also stood and we faced each other across her desk, waving our arms about. I found myself distracted by her perfume and wondered where I had smelt it before.

"Do you know what your problem is, Madam Mayor?"

"Enlighten me, Mr Goram."

"You're like all politicians – you like the power and control, you think you know what's best, but you never find out if it's what the people actually want."

She was about to reply when the door flew open and the uniformed policeman from the door ran in, his gun in his hand. "Are you alright, Madam Mayor?" he asked. "Your secretary said there was an argument, and that you were with the off-worlder who has been hanging around this morning."

"You see," I carried on, "there's all this off-worlder stuff. We're all off-worlders but you just can't see it."

Shoving past the policeman and the secretary, who was hovering in the doorway, I left, thinking that perhaps Flanagan had been right all along. Although the fact was that the place was becoming as much a society as a mining and research station. And although the vested interests might complain, there was little that could be done to stop it.

Still wound up from my argument, I walked about without knowing where I was going, trying to decide what to do. I still wanted to finish the job; in a way the official resistance had made me more determined to see it through, and to do all I could to promote the place as a tourist haunt, just to spite the establishment. I also wanted to meet Al Nichols, who might be able to tell me a bit more about Nic. Apart from Macie in the diner, I hadn't met anyone yet who didn't want to abuse me, or leave bodies in my bathroom.

I had walked quite a way from City Hall, and found myself passing a construction site; the sign said it was new offices for Balcom Industrial. The dome itself was closer but still a good hundred metres away. The more I walked around, the more I realised just how big this dome was; it had clearly been thought out with a large settlement in mind.

I knew that there was an optimum size for stress and weight bearing and of course there were other domes in the cluster but the size of this one was still impressive. As if I had known it forever, the size popped into my head: three thousand metres by eight hundred metres and forty metres high. That was a lot of enclosed space. As Macie had said, the huge weight of the structure was almost balanced by the atmospheric pressure, gravity did the rest. And this was just one dome in the cluster. I had to take a look at the dome itself. After a short walk, I found myself by it and started to look a bit more closely.

It was certainly imposing. A metal lattice frame held the hexagonal plates together, the frame painted a rusty reddish grey to match the cliffs behind, and close up the Plastoglass was tinted to reduce the light input. There were water pipes with sprinkler heads running up the frames, and rows of high-intensity lights as well.

This of course was only the inner dome – there was an air gap and an outer dome, the Plastoglass of which was twice as thick and had a liquid layer sandwiched in it. A low fence was between me and the frame, with a thin steel net attached to the metalwork to stop any objects hitting the structure. I wondered then about the policeman's gun; perhaps they fired something that wouldn't shatter the Plastoglass.

I knew that outside of the outer dome was another fine mesh net, twice as strong and capable of stopping small or medium-sized rocks. At least that was the theory. The early domes had been single skin without nets, but a major breach on Canux had been caused by a meteor the size of a grapefruit, causing consternation to say the least. A hasty rethink had led to the present design and as far as I knew, since then, no major breach had ever occurred. Inspections were continuous and sensors monitored the state of the outer net for collisions. Any object that pierced the outer dome would be slowed down by the viscous liquid layer, which was a modified form of oil, statically charged to absorb a lot of the cosmic radiation that an atmosphere and magnetic field would normally deflect. Exposed to vacuum, it solidified, sealing any breach. At least that was the plan.

I realised that I was not alone; someone had come to stand beside me.

"Have you lived under a dome before?" I turned, and a tall dark-haired woman was watching me. Her face looked vaguely familiar and her eyes had a strange look to them, as if she was miles away. Hadn't I noticed her somewhere already today?

"No, and to be honest it's freaking me out a little," I replied.

She laughed. "It's as safe as anything. I was born here and I'd feel naked without it over my head now. I couldn't imagine living somewhere and not needing it." She thought for a moment. "You should see the museum; you'll learn all about the dome and our way of life – it will help you understand a lot of things. It's free too; it's over the other side of the park." She pointed vaguely. "You can't miss it, the two weird-looking buildings."

As she walked away, I noticed her shoes: they were black with steel toecaps and a mirror shine. They didn't match her clothes, and the one thing I have learned about women is that everything should match. Maybe I was being followed after all.

The museum sounded like it might be a good place to see, so I strolled in the direction she had pointed. There in a clear space inside a low fence were two living units parked next to each other. They looked very old-fashioned. They were the sort normally used by planetary surveyors, twenty-metre long sausage-shaped things with small round windows and airlocks at each end.

They had been designed as bunk houses and living spaces for about a dozen men each. Under the accommodation were the generators and oxygen recirculators. It was a hell of a way to exist; add in working ridiculous hours and it seemed more like a prison sentence than the one I had served.

The sign over the entrance said *The Reevis Story* and I went in to find a bored old woman with a badge that said *Volunteer*. She was knitting as I came in and put it down with a guilty look. "Sorry, dear, it's for my grand-daughter," she said with a fond smile. She became the second person on Reevis, after Macie, to actually go out of their way to make me feel welcome. And the knitting seemed homely but somehow out of place in this high tec setting.

She gave me a sheaf of printed papers, dog-eared and well used, explaining that there were arrows on the floor with numbers for the exhibits relating to the notes on the paper. "If you have any questions just ask me. I'll be here," she said, as she picked up her knitting. The click of needles soon became the background to my tour. I was surprised that the information was not on a holoscreen or a headset, but figured maybe it was done the old-fashioned way to add to the experience.

It was really interesting though, and by the time I had finished looking around two hours had passed. I had a much better idea of the safety of the dome and a grudging respect for men like Harris Morgan. I had had a couple of questions about the dome and the settlement, and she had answered them in a brisk, competent voice that indicated the breadth of her knowledge.

"Do you get a lot of visitors?" I asked her on my way out, after thanking her for all her help.

"Not really, dear," she replied, sadly. "The schools come up here every so often but all the kids are interested in is getting round and out again. And we have no funding, hence the paper; we can't afford tablets and screens. Of course," she added after a second, "if that nice fellow Nic gets his hotel running a bit better, we may be rushed off our feet."

That was interesting – clearly the news hadn't spread. "Do you think he will?"

"I hope so, dear. Trouble is he gets no help from the Mayor," she pulled a face, "and all the companies seem to be against him for some reason but I think it should happen. Reevis is not just about Balcom and making money; it's such a beautiful place that everyone should have a chance to come and see it."

Walking away I realised that I was looking around and actually understanding what I was seeing. It had been a huge feat of engineering, from the digging of the kilometres of foundation to the piecing together of the framework and the layers of Plastoglass. They had actually built a small dome first, to live in whilst the larger one was being finished. And after all the building had been finished, the sealing of all the leaks and pressurising. Meanwhile a separate group were building the ancillary structures and setting up the power station to melt the ice and form the atmosphere. Then all the parts had to be linked and it all had to work.

Harris and his crew had lived here for nearly a year building the dome. Granted there had been lots of automation and several thousand people working here but it was still an enormous task. They had had disasters as well. One living unit had been hit by a meteor, losing twelve men instantly, and others had died from accidents, particularly when building the power station and diverting the lava flow. And this was not Harris Morgan's first such project either. I can only imagine the relief they must have felt when they could take their suits off.

I had also learnt that the lights set into the metal frame varied in intensity to create the illusion of day and night. In fact they were computer-controlled to replicate a sun moving across the sky in a normal Terran day. As the planet never rotated, they had a blank canvas and had opted for a Terran year, complete with seasons. As Macie had said, the breeze was a result of positive pressure and it was comforting to know that there was plenty of oxygen in the ice to keep it topped up. Not only that, the farm dome piped excess oxygen into the cluster. All the domes, but especially the farm, had extra strong and deep foundations to stop the rabbit population tunnelling their way into vacuum.

I realised that it was mid-afternoon – despite the fancy lighting my body hadn't adjusted to local time. It had gone way past when I would normally have eaten and I was feeling quite hungry, but I couldn't remember how to get back to the diner.

I spotted the dark-haired woman again; she was loitering by the edge of the grass and happened to catch my eye as I spotted her. Abruptly she looked away – was that guilt? I thought that I would confront her so I walked over to her. "Hello again," I greeted her cheerfully, "fancy seeing you here."

She gave me a funny look. "It's a small dome alright. Sorry, that's a local expression, but it's true. How did you find the museum?"

"It was very inspiring. Thanks for the suggestion," I said. "Makes you wonder how they coped all that time. But there is one thing about this place that's bothering me."

"And what's that?"

"Why is there so much anger towards off-worlders? Except for you and a couple of other people I've been made to feel about as welcome as a meteorite would be hitting the dome right now."

She looked back at me. "You've got a friendly face," was her reply, "and there are a few people on Reevis who don't agree with all the stupid polarisation. Did you see Harris Morgan's journal in the museum?"

"Yes, but I didn't look at it all."

"Well," she replied, "for me the most relevant bit was where he said, 'In the end everyone has the same enemy and it's Reevis. You may use it or live on it and even make money from it but never forget it can snuff you out without a second thought or even be aware of your passing. In a way that overrides all the petty squabbles and jealousies in its absolute truth.'"

I was stunned, trying to equate the words with the bitter

bully that I had met today. And with her memory – perhaps they taught it in school.

"The dome is Harris's baby," she continued. "Twenty years ago he conceived it and he risked everything to see it born." Her eyes had that strange look again.

"Fascinating," I said with sarcasm. "He must have changed in twenty years then, because four hours ago he called me an off-worlder and told me he would be watching me."

"Maybe he saw the suit and figured you for an office type; he's a practical man and hates people with soft hands."

"Why do you stick up for him?"

"He's my father," she said proudly. That stopped the conversation in its tracks. I let out a breath in surprise and just stood there with my mouth hanging open. "Well are you?" she persisted. "An office type."

"You're his daughter!" Somehow I hadn't imagined him as a parent; I thought he'd be too busy building worlds to settle down.

"My mother said that he told her this job would be the last, he would settle in one of his creations – after all, he expected others to. It's true that since she died he has got grumpier, but he's my father and I love him."

"I thought you were following me," was all I could think of to say.

She laughed. "Not me, I'm just having a lazy day off and you happen to be where I am."

"So what do you do then?"

She laughed again. "This is going to sound really bad, but I'm in the Reevis City Police. And what about you, Mr Off-Worlder, why are you here?"

"I'm just a poor struggling journalist, sent here on a boring job," I told her, then I had an idea. "If you're in the police, do you know an Officer Levson?"

"I'm not a proper officer," she quickly said, "I just work in the station, writing up reports and doing the filing for the detectives. I don't know all the officers by name, only the ones that I see regularly."

My stomach rumbled and I apologised. "I can't remember how to get back to the diner," I admitted, "and I'm hungry."

She got up and pointed to a dark yellow building on the other side of the park. "That's Spiro's restaurant, and he doesn't mind off-worlders. The food's pretty good too, all dome-made. I've got to get back home; nice meeting you, Mr Off-Worlder." She started to walk away.

"The name's Miles," I called after her, "Miles Goram."

"Shelly," she called back. "Enjoy your meal."

7

Sure enough Spiro's was a welcoming place, although there was only me and an elderly couple sitting inside. We nodded at each other but they were deep in conversation so I didn't intrude. I read the menu; it had a good selection of dishes and proudly proclaimed that everything on the menu was dome-made. Strangely there were no prices.

When I gave my order to the waiter, he asked me if I was on the Balcom account; when I said no he produced another menu, identical but with prices on it. I thought it might be a hike for tourists but compared to Centra it was still cheap and I realised that my expenses would cover quite a bit more than I had expected.

The look in Shelly's eyes had bothered me. Years ago, when I was a raw reporter, I had been given the job of writing about a secure hospital. The older reporters had passed the job to the junior and I soon found out why. The place was full of sad people, held for their own safety, and their stories were pathetic. Tales of past glory and injustice abounded and in my naivety I had found myself believing and sympathising with all of them. It was only afterwards, in the doctor's office, that I had learnt that the stories were just that – their delusions were the result of their mental illness. They had had eyes with the same expression as Shelly's.

I ate local lamb in a rich, fruity sauce with vegetables and finished my meal with some sort of frozen dessert. A glass of wine washed it down. It was hard to believe that all this was produced locally; the farm must be large, or just very efficient. I would go tomorrow, I decided, once I had found it. I paid and left, thinking I would walk back to the Splendid and arrange to check out. The waiter had given me directions and it seemed straightforward; after all, nowhere was far under the dome.

As I set off from the restaurant I wondered if I was still being followed and started to take more notice of the people around me. It was a lot busier, with groups of women with small children, teenagers and old-timers, all milling around with no apparent purpose. It must have been the end of the working day. Looking around me I was still unable to spot anyone obvious. The feeling grew, and I started to dodge about and double back, trying to spot patterns in the people around me, until I was disorientated and starting to panic.

I ducked down an alleyway between two large buildings; it was one of the few places in Reevis where I had seen deep shadow. The floor was strewn with old papers and the remains of takeaway food. I thought I heard a small animal scuttle, would there be rats here? The walls on either side of me were windowless, and as I walked quickly I heard my steps echo. Then I noticed another echo, from more feet. I turned, and there were two people walking towards me. I started walking again, slightly faster. I could see the end of the alley, brightly lit, when a figure appeared, blocking my exit. The two behind me sped up until I was trapped. I almost ran, but somehow kept walking, until my way was blocked.

"Let me past," I said to the mountain in front of me. He stood silently, shaking his head. He wore the same overalls as the group I had seen in the diner, with the Balcom jacket and heavy boots. Thick leather gauntlets were pushed through his belt. I thought that I could feel the breath of the two behind me, hot on my collar, they were pressed in that close without actually touching me. His helmeted head had a tinted visor pulled down so his features were impossible to see clearly but

I thought he was one of the men who had been with Harris in the diner.

"A word of advice," one of the two behind me said, "stop your meddling and leave."

"I suppose Harris sent you," I replied, trying to sound calm. "Have I upset him?"

"Never mind who sent us," growled a different voice. "Things here don't concern you; a good journalist knows when to cut his losses."

"Or else?" I said. The man in front of me just flexed his shoulders; it was an impressive sight and made the point without words.

"How are we all today?" The unexpected question also came from behind me, in a young voice, and suddenly the two pushed past me, shoving me to the ground in their eagerness to get out into the open. When I got back up, all three men had vanished and I was being watched by two teenagers, dressed in identical purple jackets. I got up and made my way out into the sunlight; there were more teenagers in a group and we were joined by the one who had been behind me.

"Who are you lot?" I asked in confusion. This place seemed to be a mix of conflicting groups, all with their own agenda.

"We call ourselves the Rangers," said the oldest, a clean-cut boy of around seventeen, with cropped blond hair. "We're from the Academy." He gestured at the jackets, which bore a crest on the breast pocket. "We look out for off-worlders being threatened, unofficially of course. An off-worlder isn't a popular thing to be around Reevis City. We try to keep the Balcom squad company, safety in numbers and all that."

I shook my head. "I can't believe this place; everything here is so polarised." There was laughter from the group.

A girl spoke up from the back, "You won't believe it but things are better now." She forced her way to the front, a small, dark-haired, intense person with glasses. "There's a real aversion to change from some of the old hands. They seem to think that Reevis is only for Balcom and its tame subjects, anyone else is not wanted." There were murmurs of agreement. "Once you've been here a few years or do something they consider useful you're tolerated, but anyone who rocks the boat is in all sorts of trouble."

"Balcom sees non-essentials as a waste of their resources," shouted a voice from the back and there were more murmurs of agreement.

"As if it was all theirs anyway," shouted another.

"Well," I said, "I don't threaten easily, but I don't think I can leave till the police have finished with me."

"You mean about Nic's murder?" said the boy, and she kicked his shins, dark eyes looking bigger under the thick lenses.

"Shhh, Lance, we're not supposed to know that." She turned to me, "What were you doing in that alleyway?" Her tone was accusing, as if I'd been silly. According to the desk clerk, I suppose I had been.

"I thought I was being followed," I said, "so I dodged down there to get away. I've got a job to do and people keep trying to warn me off. To be honest I'm starting to get fed up with it. So I'm going to carry on and do it, because that seems to be the thing that will upset most of them."

"Fair enough," she said, "just who have you been upsetting? We know they were Balcom heavies just now."

I told them about the Mayor and Harris Morgan and there were several shouts of abuse at the mention of the names. "Well," she said, "if you're set on staying my advice is to let us help you blend in."

I had the feeling that I was being rushed. It was just another kind of threat in its way, sort of disguised with apparent kindness.

"That's good of you," I said cautiously. "Is this what you do then, just hang around in dark alleys helping people?"

"We have an agenda as much as they do," she replied. "We want Reevis to be open. Do you know how hard it is to leave here without Balcom's say so, about the censorship of the video, or all the other petty restrictions on life? You're important – you're the first journalist that's been here for ages, we need you to go back and report what's going on."

It seemed to me that everyone wanted different things from me: Nic wanted me to say how good Reevis was, and these vigilantes wanted me to say how bad. And the Mayor and Balcom wanted me gone. Caught up in a maze of conflicting pressures I shrugged my shoulders and went with them.

We ended up at someone's house where I was given a black holdall. When I opened it, I could see overalls and a helmet and I guessed that there were other things as well. The girl zipped it shut. "These will keep you from being so conspicuous," she said. "We'll walk with you back to the Splendid, and be there in the morning. What's your plan for tomorrow?"

I didn't particularly want to share my plans with them, but as they could always join the throng and follow me, I told them, "I'm off to the farm. I want to see Nic's hotel – I've still got a review to write and I want to meet someone called Al."

"That's Al Nichols," one of the group said. "He does these amazing tours, hot and cold sides."

"I've never been," said another, "all we ever do is go to the museum of knitting." There was laughter.

"Do you think they'll try to warn me off again then?" I thought that once they knew these Rangers were around they might back off.

"It's not just Balcom – the Mayor's secret police are following you as well. The Balcom boys will leave you alone if we're around. But once you get out of this dome, it's a different world."

The boy, Lance, and the girl, whose name was Jennie, walked with me back to the Splendid. The lights were dimmer now and the artificial early evening had a crimson glow. "One of us will see you in the morning," Lance said, "and take you to the farm." I thanked them and went inside.

The same man was on the desk, reading the same magazine. "Hi," he greeted me, "back for a few more room changes are we?"

"I hope not; I could do with a quiet night. Don't you ever have time off?"

"Not me," he replied, "I love it here." The sarcasm was not lost on me. "How did you get on in our lovely town?"

"Well I nearly got beaten up twice, run over once and the locals were mostly rude, but I had an interesting day for all that."

"Is your life always like this?" He sounded jealous.

I had barely had time to get up the stairs to my room and unzip the holdall when the door buzzed. I crammed the overalls back in the holdall and went to the door.

Flanagan was outside. "Buy you a beer?" he suggested. Back down the stairs again.

8

The shutters were up and the bar was doing a roaring trade, construction workers seeing how much beer they could drink. The restaurant was quiet though and we sat at a corner table. I ordered us both a beer and asked for a platter of sandwiches, Flanagan asked the waiter for some peanuts.

"Peanuts?" I said in shock. Was there no limit to the variety of local produce? They came in an opaque foil bag; 'Roasted and Salted, Dome-Made Peanuts' it said proudly.

"They grow them on the farm," he explained, shaking a few out of the packet and putting them in his mouth. He chewed and swallowed. "What have you been up to today, then?"

Seeing the look on my face he added, "Don't worry, this is not an official interrogation, just a conversation." I had the feeling that wasn't strictly true; it may be unofficial but he wouldn't miss much, and his matey attitude was probably a way of getting information the polite way. But if Lance was right, my movements were all on CCTV and the secret police had me taped, so I probably couldn't be invisible if I tried.

"I nearly got run over because you all drive on the left here," Flanagan grinned at this, "had a coffee in the diner, got into an argument with someone called Harris Morgan, and then I saw the Mayor. Then I had another argument with Harris Morgan and took a look around the dome and the museum. I also met someone who claimed to be Harris Morgan's daughter."

He looked blank, then said, "Oh, you have been busy."

My food had arrived while I was speaking and it looked pretty good, a mixture of cheese and ham sandwiches with salad and some pickles on a tray. I started eating as Flanagan sipped his beer. The sandwiches were really good; the bread was fresh and crusty and the fillings excellent.

"Hmm, quite a day then. So how did your visit with our Mayor go?" he asked.

"Pretty much as you hinted," I mumbled as I chewed. "The Mayor takes the corporate line; she seemed cosy with Harris Morgan."

Flanagan nodded. "So you met him. He was one of the first to set foot on Reevis," he grinned. "An old-fashioned pioneer, but not always a particularly nice one."

"I found that out," I told him, and gave him the gist of our meetings, including the one in the alley. "Although he wasn't there," I added.

"We think he stirs up a lot of the anti-off-worlder sentiment," he agreed, "but never openly. It's all done through others; his hands are clean." He paused. "You met the Rangers as well, I guess?"

I hadn't told him about their part in the confrontation in the alley, but I did now. He nodded. "Sounds about right, just about all the newcomers get that sort of treatment."

In a way I thought that it was a good thing that Nic had built his hotel in the farm. It would keep the tourists insulated from the atmosphere in the main dome. "So how did you know about the Rangers?" I asked. "Don't tell me you've been following me as well as everyone else?"

Once again he didn't answer all my question. "I saw you come back in, you had a black holdall." I just looked at him. "OK," he grinned, "I've not got X-Ray eyes, I saw Lance and Jennie following you, and the black holdall is kind of a trademark." He waved his empty bottle at the waitress, who nodded.

"What's the official line on the Rangers?"

The beers arrived and he took a swig, followed by more peanuts. "Well they are officially frowned on – after all, I'm the law, not some bunch of kids – but actually we're fairly sympathetic. They do stop a lot of the intimidation; just being around makes them witnesses. Their parents don't always like it of course, but none of them has ever been hurt."

"They told me that Balcom controlled the video, and stopped people travelling – is that true?"

"No," he shook his head, "that's a bit over the top. Sure it's their satellite for comms and video but apart from the data privacy and usual filters, I don't think it's sinister. And as far as I know, there's free movement for anyone not working on sensitive projects. But they knew that when they signed up," he added quickly.

"So the Rangers are just another faction with an agenda?"

"The Rangers are like any other gang, some of its true and some are attempting to justify their position." He looked at his watch and drained his beer. "Sorry, I got to go. Keep safe, and don't believe everything you hear." And with that he was gone.

I ate the last sandwich and finished up my beer. I debated having another drink and decided against it. Once I got back to my room, I got out my tablet and played the rest of the drive. After Nic's words 'and there's more' I was expecting a lot, so I was disappointed to find that there were just some grainy CCTV pictures of Layla entering the main dome. The rest of the drive was full of copies of the security and immigration logs that didn't match up with the pictures, and Nic's questioning of why none of this was featured in any official investigation.

I decided to try to contact Gaynor. Even after Flanagan's reassurances, I was conscious that all the communication systems were controlled and built by Balcom, so I didn't want to say anything too sensitive. My tablet said that with the time difference, it would be the middle of the night on Centra, so in the end I just sent her a message to say that I had arrived OK but there were complications and I would be in touch.

After that there was nothing else to do. I looked out of the window; the lighting had reduced to minimum, the only illumination the rosy glow from behind the cliffs. Reevis City slept, maybe not the sleep of the just, but everyone that I had met today certainly believed it of their cause. I turned in for the night and surprisingly I slept well.

Next morning, after a shower and breakfast, I returned to my room and changed into the clothes from the holdall, a clean but worn orange boiler suit with a black and yellow Balcom jacket over it, boots with hardened toecaps and a hard hat with a visor. I pushed the visor up and looked in the mirror and the helmet, along with the fact that I hadn't shaved, made quite a difference to my appearance. I put my regular clothes and valuables in the holdall and carried it downstairs with me. The desk clerk never gave me a second look.

As I left the hotel, Lance joined me. "Pretty good," he said, "at least from a distance, but you still walk like an office worker."

I felt insulted; I was trying my best. "How do you mean?"

"Well you have to wear it like you're used to working in it." I dropped my shoulders and imagined that the holdall was heavy. "That's better," he grinned.

"You said last night that the secret police were following me – how can you know that?"

"We know who they are," he admitted, "or at least Jennie thinks that she does; she spotted them around you yesterday. I suppose that doesn't make them very secret, but it keeps the general population on their toes, sort of 'we know that you know that we know'."

"I guess it's a bit of a waste of time trying to shake them off, then?"

"Well if you're going to Nic's hotel, there are cameras on all the exits so you're going to be spotted. Anyhow that's what they expect you to do, isn't it." And that was very true. Lance walked me over to the airlock. He told me that the authorities had got more repressive over the last year or so; his father had wanted to take the family to Drylax, one of the pleasure planets, to celebrate Lance's exam results, but had been refused permission because he was engaged on sensitive work. That tied in with what Flanagan had told me and then he said, "It was strange, because he's a shift supervisor at the power plant, he monitors the ice converters and electrolysis gear."

"That doesn't sound like sensitive work." I was puzzled.

"No," he agreed, "it doesn't, but only a week before he was critical of some of the changes to working practices in the plant. He sent a message to the manager saying that there were too many reductions in safety, and it would never have happened before Tony Hays became Balcom's top man on Reevis."

"That seems a little co-incidental," I said.

"Yes," he agreed, "and my mother couldn't take us without him either, same reason."

That was the first time I had heard the name Tony Hays. It was another piece in the puzzle that was Reevis.

"The airlock is just over there," said Lance. "I'll be off now. You'll find it different once you get out of this dome."

I turned to thank him, but he had already gone.

9

I reached the airlock and was surprised to find that it wasn't attached to the dome, but was situated well inside it. There was a wide doorway, large enough for a trailer to get through, under an arched building. The entrance was closed with a heavy metallic door. The lock was manned by a bored-looking old man in a stained boiler suit. He was sitting in front of a holoscreen complete with a virtual control panel hovering in the air. Looking a bit closer, I saw that he only had one arm. He looked at my overalls and bag through his screen, showing no interest.

"You wanna go through to the hub?" He didn't ask for any sort of pass, which was a good job; perhaps the clothes were enough.

"Yeah, I'm going to the farm," I replied and he shrugged.

"Whatever, as if I care. Balcom goes where they like." He checked a readout on his screen. "Pressure's good in the tubes," he chuckled, "always an advantage." He pressed buttons on the virtual panel and the door slid down into the ground. "See you later," he called as I walked through. I waved at him and the door hissed shut behind me.

The building covered a gently sloping ramp that went down into a round chamber about twenty metres across, lined with metal. Bright lights hung from the ceiling. On the opposite side was an opening, a wide black hole leading who knows where. There were two open-topped runarounds parked in marked bays on the opposite side of the space to the opening; the drivers were talking. When they saw me the nearest one shouted over to me: "Where you off to?"

"I'm going to the farm," I answered.

"Jump in then. I'm Lou," he said, waving his hand over his shoulder to the seats in the rear. I did and he started up the engine. It rattled for a bit like it was going to explode.

"Don't worry," he shouted over his shoulder, "methane engines need to warm up to run smooth." Sure enough the engine note settled and we drove into the tunnel. There was no fixed lighting and he turned on powerful lamps on the front of his vehicle. We carried on in a dead straight line for a couple of minutes; in the dark enclosed space, it felt as if we were moving really fast as the metal bulkheads flashed by. Every few hundred metres there were wider places where two vehicles could pass, with lights indicating clearance to proceed or stop. We waited in one place at a red light and a large lorry came past, towing two trailers.

"Are you new here," asked Lou, looking at my overalls.

"Yes that's right," I replied. I hoped he didn't ask me anything specific, it would be obvious that I wasn't a Balcom employee straight away. Instead he just nodded.

"Bet you've not seen a place like this before then, let me explain, that's a load of food from the farm, there are sensors all along the tunnel; they control the lights and the traffic." The light turned green and we carried on.

After about a minute we passed a green light and popped out into a replica of the chamber we had just left, only much larger. There was a stand selling food and drink and a whole load of parked vehicles of all descriptions. They were parked in the middle of the space; the road went around the outside in a circle. I thought that we would stop but we kept on and plunged into another tunnel.

"That was the hub," said Lou, "all the domes connect to the hub. We are now approaching the farm." Sure enough, after another passing place we started up a slope and popped out in a small dome above ground. The runaround stopped.

"Here we are, the farm," he said.

"How much is that?" I asked but he waved me away.

"There's no charge for Balcom workers, didn't they tell you? If you were an off-worlder it would be on the meter, but Balcom pay us a monthly fee for transits. If there's no one here when you're done, there's a call button by the door. You have a good day."

I thanked him and he spun the vehicle around, revved the engine and disappeared back into the tunnel. After the events of yesterday, the thought that I had got something from Balcom cheered me up.

This dome was a lot smaller and the glass was not polarised. Through it I could see the blaze of stars in one direction and the glow of the sun in the other, as well as the outside of a huge dome that must be the farm.

After a short walk along another passageway, I reached a lock with a door that opened as I approached. There was no one around, then I saw the camera and realised that it was remote. I stepped through and it slid shut behind me. I was bathed in blue light and sprayed with a mist of something that had a chemical tang. I also had to walk through a trough of liquid.

A voice over a loudspeaker explained that it was a special disinfecting process designed to keep the bacteria strains in the farm pure. He asked me to empty my bag out and have the contents sprayed as well. When the spraying had finished a blast of warm air dried me off in no time and I repacked my gear. "OK," said the voice, "you're done. Walk towards the door." As I did it opened.

I walked through into another world. This end of the dome was less in the shadow of the crater edge, and the glow in the sky was stronger. The material of the dome was less polarised, probably to help the plants grow, and the lights shining from the frame were much brighter. A network of pipes hung from the frame about ten metres high and water dripped.

To my left the road was signposted 'Processing Plant and Co-Operative Offices'. To my right it said 'Hotel and Accommodation'. I turned right.

The road led between fields; to my left there was some sort of grain waving in a light breeze provided by a bank of fans and to my right a fenced paddock of mixed animals. They grazed on bright green grass, or sat chewing under spreading fruit trees. Bees and small birds flitted, setting up a background hum. The air smelt of damp earth. As I walked down the roadway, tractors and harvesting machinery passed me, the drivers waving and smiling. It seemed as if I had returned to Terra, or some other agricultural world.

This dome seemed huge, maybe because of the lack of buildings in the middle. I walked on, towards a wide, squat building tucked away at the edge of the space nearest the cliffs. It was made of a pale grey material. As I got closer, I could see that it was made of local stone that had been cut into bricks, unlike the extruded polymers and metals of the buildings in the main dome.

As I went inside, I could see that the hotel was about as different to my current abode as could be, with thick carpeting and lots of real wood panelling in the vestibule. There had obviously been no expense spared in its construction. The desk was impressive: a single block of stone straight from the quarry, with rough edges but a machine-smooth top. Uniformed staff scuttled about.

"Hello, sir," said the desk clerk, tail-suited and wearing white gloves. He was not reading a magazine like his counterpart but was attentive and friendly. "Welcome to the Hotel Stavriedies, how can I help you?"

"I would like a room, please."

"Of course, sir," he said. "May I see an ID, please?" I handed it over. "Ah, Mr Goram, Nic said that you would be along, although we expected you a few days ago. I'm afraid that Nic isn't here at the moment, but I will make sure he knows you have arrived." He appeared unaware of Nic's fate, or maybe he thought it might be bad for business to broadcast the fact. I didn't know whether to tell him or not. I decided not.

"I've been staying at the Splendid," I told him, and he shuddered.

"That's unfortunate," he answered, straight-faced while looking at my clean but worn working clothes. "We can get your possessions brought over." He made a note on his screen. "Nic has instructed us to keep a room for you."

I didn't like the preferential treatment. Not that I minded being pampered, but I was here to write a review. It occurred to me that this might have been deliberate, to get a good write up, but on the other hand, it may be how they treated all the guests. I would have to keep my eyes open and try to be impartial.

He gave me a key card and I declined the offer of a man to carry my single bag for me. I took the lift up to the sixth floor. As the lift worked in this hotel, it was already ahead of the Splendid on points. The lift was carpeted and immaculately clean. Muzak played quietly. The air smelt faintly of sandalwood.

Stopping on the sixth floor, the doors opened to a wide corridor with windows at each end. My feet made no sound as I walked towards my room across the thick carpet. There was a trolley full of linen, towels and assorted cleaning products parked outside the room next to mine. I opened the door and stepped into my new home.

I dropped the holdall and my jaw went with it. The room was like a palace. There were several deep armchairs arranged around a low table, a long sofa against one wall and the biggest bed I had seen outside my penthouse flat. There was a tall fridge in the corner and when I opened it, there were bottles of champagne, beers, spirits and various snacks.

I knew that the hotel was intended for high-end tourists, but this was opulence on a grand scale. Feeling out of place in my overalls and jacket, I changed into the casual clothes I had brought in the holdall and stashed my valuables in the safe. The bathroom was as big as the whole room in the Splendid – no sliding doors here, just a rack of expensive toiletries and fluffy towels.

Reluctantly I left this paradise and went in search of the bar. It was on the top floor and like the Splendid was combined with the restaurant. But that was where the similarity ended.

In keeping with the rest of the place, it was plush and welcoming; the whole three-sixty degrees of the wall and roof were Plastoglass in the familiar hexagonal panels, giving an uninterrupted view over the sea of waving crops in one direction and the cliffs in the other.

I realised that the back wall of the hotel was the wall of the dome itself. Red light played around the outline of the cliffs looming over us, giving the impression of a wild pyrotechnic party on the other side. Looking down through this wall I could see several moderately sized side domes and a line of pipes heading into the cliffs. There were tables set out over the floor, with a few groups of people sitting around in comfortable-looking chairs, eating, drinking and chatting. A four-piece band was playing restrained jazz music. Everyone looked prosperous and relaxed.

The bar was circular and set in the middle of the room, with televisor screens hung over the stools, although why anyone would want to watch sports with the show outside I wasn't sure. Maybe if you saw it every day it would get boring, but I hadn't been here long enough for that, and if I was lucky, I wouldn't be here much longer.

I took off my jacket and sat on a stool at the bar. Immediately a uniformed barman appeared with ice water and an attentive air; he couldn't know why I was here so maybe it wasn't special treatment after all. I ordered a local beer, the same as I had drunk with Flanagan yesterday back at the Splendid. That was a time that was already receding into my past, to be filed under 'Things never to do again'.

My beer arrived in short time, dew drops shining on the cool glass, along with a small dish of peanuts. I thought of Flanagan and as I tried a few I wondered what he would make of this place. The beer was just as good too, and I was just considering whether it was too early to have another when a man slipped onto the stool next to me. He waved at the barman and turned to me with his hand outstretched.

"You must be Miles Goram; the duty manager said you'd turned up. I'm Al Nichols. I understand that you were here to see Nic."

10

Al Nichols was tall and thin, with short blond hair. His movements were jerky and urgent, and he spoke in the same way. His suit was two sizes too big and hung off his angular frame. His handshake was stronger than his size suggested and I saw steel in his bright blue eyes, where I also saw warmth.

"You got here quickly," I said.

"Ahh well," he replied, "we've been expecting you for a couple of days and my office is just off the back of the lobby. Roddy on the desk tipped me off." A tall glass of something with ice chinking was placed in front of him, and another beer appeared in front of me. "Thanks, Gaz," he said to the barman. "This is Miles – if he comes in here, give him as much beer as he wants, on my tab."

Gaz nodded. "Yes, Mr Al," he said as Al swallowed half his glass in one. "First today," he said appreciatively, "well, from this glass, anyhow. Your health."

"Thanks, and yours," I replied, clicking his glass with my bottle. He looked at me as if he expected me to speak. Better get on with it, I thought, so taking a mental deep breath I asked the burning question. "Sorry to be blunt but do you know about Nic?"

I couldn't be sure if he knew; the man at the desk hadn't, or hadn't said. It seemed that the news might have reached some but not others. He nodded and suddenly I saw devastation in those eyes.

"Oh yes, I know, and despite my initial thoughts, I also know that you have a cast-iron alibi. Nic had a few friends in the town dome but he never used to go there much if he could help it. So when he went, we assumed that it was because you had arrived and called him."

"So you didn't know about the delay on the shuttle."

He shook his head. "Only after Nic had gone. The news was off, satellite problems, and Gaz spotted that there had been a delay when the feed came back on. We figured Nic would be back here as soon as he got to the port and found you hadn't landed. But he didn't show up and then his phone went dead. Next thing we got a visit from some Detective Chimney or something to give us the news."

"That would be Chumna," I told him, "short, round and a bit scruffy."

"That's him," he agreed.

"Him and his mate gave me the once-over after they found his body," I said, "then the room they moved me to was trashed while I was at breakfast."

He looked suitably shocked. "I'm not surprised. I know there was something Nic wanted to give you and I'd told him he should be careful." He was waving his arms about to make his point. "Some files or video or something, he probably kept it on his phone, which, as I said, is missing."

"I found his jacket in the hotel room, at least my first one," I told him. "It had your card in the pocket. Obviously I was coming over here anyway, for the review."

He hadn't heard me and carried on talking about Nic. "So Nic must have gone to the hotel," he said. "That's interesting."

"Didn't the police tell you he was found in my room? Didn't they give you any details?"

"Not about where he was found, no, the detective only said that he was dead; he didn't say where or how."

"He was in the bathroom of my hotel room; he'd been strangled. I thought I was going to be a suspect. If the shuttle hadn't been delayed then I guess I would have been." It also occurred to me that if the shuttle hadn't been delayed I could have been laid out on the bathroom floor with him.

He looked at me, and I could almost see the wheels going round in his head. He seemed to be wrestling with a decision and I kept quiet and sipped my beer, looking out at the cliffs over his shoulder.

As we had been speaking, the red glow behind the cliffs had become more intense and waves of crimson clouds were ascending into the black sky. Shot through with pink and scarlet they looked like the aurora on Terra as they faded and reappeared. There was a collective groan as all the video screens went blank.

"More solar wind." Gaz was talking to a couple at the other end of the bar: "The cosmic rays energise the radiated particles from the lava, and it sparkles." They oohed and ahhed at the sight. "Unfortunately it means no communications for a day or so," he continued, "the satellites shut down again."

"That or Balcom's got something new to hide," Al muttered. "Come on then." He drained his drink, got up and walked to the lifts. I followed. I guessed that he had made his mind up.

We left the bar and went back down to the lobby in silence. Al turned to the side of the desk, where I saw a sign in glowing neon: 'AL'S TOURS. SEE THE WONDERS OF REEVIS,' and an arrow. A short passage led to a room like a departure lounge, where there was a huge 3D video screen showing film taken from the front of one of his vehicles. It looked exciting as the camera bounced around, showing grey rock, then stars then flashes of red. It almost gave me motion sickness. It might have persuaded some people to take the tour, but I was not one of them.

A young woman was seated behind the desk typing on a keypad. She looked up as we approached, showing wide violet eyes and a generous application of lipstick and eyeliner.

I suddenly realised that she was almost the first woman I had seen on the planet this heavily made-up. The female population on Reevis seemed to prefer the scrubbed natural look that you never see on the more boring or conventional worlds. "Hi," she said to Al in a tone that suggested more than a working relationship, then she turned to me and I felt myself being scrutinised.

"Hi, May," said Al, "this is Miles; he's the writer that Nic was on about, rest him."

She smiled at me, a sad smile. "You poor thing, all this happening and when you've only just got here. Nic was such a fine man. Wait a minute," she said, "I recognise you – you're that gossip columnist right?"

"I used to be," I agreed, "but now I just tell the truth."

She laughed, "That's not your reputation. People always said you were the most honest of the bunch."

"Thanks." I smiled, but she had gone back to her task. I could see a tear on her face.

Off to one side was an office; we went in and Al closed and locked the door. It suddenly reminded me of the first time my cell door had shut behind me, sealing me in with someone I didn't know, and I was overwhelmed by panic.

"Don't lock me in! I can't take it," I shouted, my voice cracked and squeaking.

Al went pale. "Sorry," he said, and he turned and flipped the lock as someone knocked heavily on the door, shouting, "Are you OK?"

"I should have realised. I just wanted privacy to tell you this." He opened the door. "May," he called, "it's alright; just turn off the sign and buzz if anyone comes down." He pulled the door almost shut, leaving a slight gap. "How's that?"

"No, I'm sorry. I can't help it, though. I thought I was over it but every now and then the sound of a door locking brings it all back." In my mind I saw the back of the cell door, cream paint and rust, with letters carved on it by previous inmates. I felt how I felt when I had been deprived of my freedom and the injustice of it all. "It's the one thing every prisoner hates, that sound. But it's even worse for the ones who know that they are innocent."

Al had listened to my anguished voice in silence. "But you were, and you were released." I nodded and sat in an armchair, Al sat behind his desk.

"Nic was killed to shut him up," he announced without preamble, "and if you hadn't been delayed you would probably have been as well."

"The thought has crossed my mind. Flanagan and the Mayor both said he wasn't popular. Have you got any suspects?"

He laughed. "You haven't been here long, have you?"

"Just long enough to know that everyone dislikes everyone else."

"OK," he smiled, "perhaps you can see it, so you'll realise that the list isn't short. About the only one not on it is you at the moment."

I felt relieved. "Nic wasn't an off-worlder too was he?"

"No," he said, "Nic was a Balcom software engineer, but he said the wrong thing to the wrong person. There's been a lot of that recently."

I thought of the information Nic had on the drive; it was certainly enough to have got him killed. And I thought of what Lance had told me this morning. There was a story here all right, just not the one I had thought I was coming to tell. I wished that the old me, the fearless one with clout was still around, not the frightened powerless me that I was now. Between us we'd soon have had the answers. The moment passed.

"What about you?" I asked him, back in bored journalist mode. "Were you Balcom as well?"

"Nope," he said in a way that suggested relief, "I was

federal. The dome was originally a federal project, but they needed a commercial partner to help spend the taxpayers' cash and Balcom got the job, mainly because of their experience. Harris Morgan, ignorant little oaf that he is, pretty much wrote the book on domes."

"And what about you then?" I still couldn't imagine how he fitted in.

"Well I got here when the dome was completed – not this dome, the first one. I was with the terraformers, so I'm officially not an off-worlder, but because I was never a Balcom man and I went into partnership with the farmers, I'm not liked. And there's the thing with the pigeons."

I'd done a piece about terraformers once: they were planet engineers, they made places liveable, a short phrase but covering an unbelievable number of skills. In short they created habitable conditions by modifying planets to enable life. A lot of their work was long term – changing a planet's ecosystem couldn't always be rushed – but on Reevis, making a town in a dome would have been child's play. "What about the pigeons?"

"That's an ecology thing – to complete the ecosystem we needed animal life. We had bees for pollination, the soil was full of worms and bacteria, there were mice and cats and rabbits but we needed birdlife to balance things. Pigeons are as good as anything – they're tough and you can always eat them if times get hard. And they help build up the flora, transporting seeds around in their gut. And then there's the waste product, a good fertiliser. Trouble is we didn't include a suitable predator so they multiplied, and it got out of hand. I got the blame for not choosing a smaller bird." He laughed. "But in the end I did get some birds of prey out here – I saved a species of hawk from extinction actually – and pigeon pie is always on the menu. Behind my back I'm known as the Birdman of Reevis, amongst other, less complimentary things."

Al had given me more pieces of the puzzle, and I was starting to get a feel for the situation on Reevis. It was a lot more complex than I had expected. And even though I'd only just met him, I couldn't help but like him.

"I'll have to take you outside the dome," said Al, "I can give you the grand tour. My base is in a side dome."

"That sounds good," I said automatically, but in reality I was concerned about being outside. Once again it was the fear of vacuum.

"But not today," he added, to my relief, "I've got too much on." He thought for a moment. "I've got to go out tomorrow – you can come along. Be in the lobby at six am and we'll go up to the lookout."

That would give me the rest of today to psych myself up. "Fine," I said, "if you're busy now I can have a look round the farm, do a bit of background."

"That would be a good idea. Sorry, but I've got a bit of stuff to do. Hang on," he took out his phone and dialled a number. "Hello, Davis," he said, "I've got Miles Goram here. Yes, the journalist. Can you look after him, show him around the place? OK, thanks." He turned to me: "Davis Muloy, the farm manager, is coming over; he'll take you round and tell you all about it."

"I forgot you run the farm as well, thanks, Al. I'll go back upstairs and put my overalls back on."

"Not a problem, Miles, he'll be in the lobby when you get back down. He's a good man, and he'll look after you. See you in the morning." He picked up a bundle of papers as I left the room.

May gave me a sympathetic look. "Are you alright, Mr Goram?" she enquired. "Can I get you anything?"

"I'm fine thanks, I just get a bit worried in enclosed spaces."

"I expect you do," she said. "I know what you went through and I think it was terrible, all those lies."

11

I went back up to my room; housekeeping were still in the corridor, the trolley had moved a little. They had been in my room as my bag had been moved from the bed onto the floor. I put my overalls and boots back on and returned to the lobby.

When I got out of the lift I saw a man in a white lab coat sitting in a chair, reading from a holoscreen. When he saw me he got up. "I'm Davis Muloy," he introduced himself. "Al asked me to show you around. Ask whatever you want and I'll do my best to tell you."

He had a small vehicle outside, a bit like a tractor with heavy tyres and an open cab; we climbed in and set off towards the other end of the dome.

Davis told me that the farm dome was four thousand metres across and elliptical in shape. That made it slightly bigger than the main dome. With the hotel in one lobe and accommodation and factories in the other, it left the rest for crops and livestock. We drove along a roadway carved between fields of wheat, corn, beans and potatoes. The air was clean and insects flitted, the breeze made a rustling noise amongst the plants. We met people working, either on foot or riding tractors; they all waved and greeted us. Davis stopped and spoke to them all and they were happy to share their knowledge with me. It was such a change from the sense of fear in the main dome that I found myself chatting to more and more of them as we drove around, the snippets of information they gave me adding to the facts I had already picked up.

"We can grow a crop every ninety days," one man told

me, "and rotate the pigs and the plants. They fertilise the soil and dig it up for us, which saves us a lot of ploughing."

"The cows and sheep live in the orchards – it saves space," said another, laughing. "But we have to be quick picking the fruit."

We arrived at the other end and went into the buildings. There was a slaughterhouse and meat processor, a milking shed and dairy, along with vegetable packers and a brewery. It was amazing just what was produced in this one dome.

"How can you get the diversity of produce in such a small space?" I asked Davis.

"We have multiple crops and companion planting," he told me, "and because we can vary the light and control the irrigation we can get things to maturity really quickly. All except the livestock, but we graze them all over and have quite a few in total so the turnover is there."

I asked him about the specialised products that I had seen.

"We grow hydroponically in the side domes," he said. "All the quick crops and the more intensive and complicated stuff where we can micro-control the environment, you'll see."

Sure enough, off to the rear there were a series of smaller domes, each with its own climate control. Some had soil-based systems for cocoa and nuts, whilst others had what Davis described as vertical farms. These were racks of tanks with plants growing out of them. The racks rotated towards the ceiling lights on a chain and rail system so they all got equal light. It was a very clever way of maximising crops in the space. Water splashed down in a cascade from tank to tank.

"The ice is surprisingly rich in minerals and nutrients," Davis said. "If the planet had rotated and maybe been a bit further from the star, life could have evolved here."

There were fish in the tanks. "They help distribute nutri-ents and we feed them worms from the compost system, then we eat them – it's a good way to use everything."

I asked a man in a white coat about the seafood I had seen in the store. "Come with me." He invited me through the racks of plants into another dome. This one was quite large and had tanks of water with fish and shellfish inside. Some were sunk into the ground, while others were suspended in rows on shelving. Pumps hummed, circulating water and feeders hung over the tanks, dribbling food to the hungry mouths below.

"We're really proud of this," he said, "and it was all Nic's idea; he brought a few fish and some oysters back ages ago and we managed to keep them going, now they're our biggest sellers. But this is the best bit." At the back was a huge black-sided tank. Mounted on hydraulics it moved about with a life of its own. At least ten metres square and five deep, you could hear the water moving about in it. "Look up," said the man. There was a mirror over the tank and in it I could see a lot of large fish. I did a double take.

"They're salmon!" I exclaimed.

"That's right," Davis proudly replied, "the motion simulates the waves in the sea, the water's saline, and they love it."

We sat down for a meal with all the staff that were not busy; there were about twenty of them round a large table, and they all chattered and passed bowls and platters around, treating me like one of the team. The food was a collection of all the offcuts and slight second-quality stuff from the processors.

"The perfect quality stuff goes for sale to the hotels, restaurants and shops," the man sitting next to me explained, as he passed a bowl of crisp salad leaves, "and then what's left is shared between the staff here and the corporate customers like the council and Balcom. There's nothing wrong with any of it, it's just not quite perfect."

"We also pack long-life rations for the guys working

outside," said another man. "We try to make them special cos the people are stuck miles from anywhere, so we know that at least they'll get a good meal."

"Balcom used to buy the best for their staff," interrupted one of the women, "until Tony Hays got his hands on the figures. Now the executives have the best and the workers get the slight seconds; they tried to get us to cut the quality in the ration packs to save money but we take the hit on them because it just seemed like the right thing to do."

The food once again was superb. If this was not the top quality stuff then I had been living on scraps so far, it was so much better than any food I had ever tasted.

"Of course a lot of it was only harvested yesterday," Davis carried on. "We rotate the crops and keep storage to a minimum. That's Gina's problem." He waved to a green-haired girl who was gazing at a holoscreen whilst she was eating, her hand going through the picture every time she took a mouthful. She nodded to herself and typed as she ate, totally absorbed. "You can't stop her working," he explained, "she's like that all day."

"And half the night," shouted a bearded man sitting next to her and everyone laughed.

"That's her husband," Davis explained and she punched him lightly on the shoulder with the hand that she wasn't typing with, her flow uninterrupted.

After we had all finished, Davis took me through the processing plant, where the raw materials were turned into food. There was a mill for the grains, along with a space where beer and wine were being fermented. Next to them was a bakery, a butchers and a dairy, with a milking parlour. Near the end was a pack house and freeze dryer. The whole place was a model of efficiency, with white-coated workers and gleaming metal machinery. Tucked away in the corner was a storage warehouse.

"What do you think about our little set-up then?" asked Davis, as we returned to his vehicle.

"I'm really impressed; you seem to have thought of everything. You must make a good profit."

He smiled, "We don't do too badly. A few of the tourists want us to export to their worlds."

"I'm not surprised. Your stuff is good but surely that would make it too expensive."

"That's what we reckoned at first. Gina looked into it and we would have to double our volumes to get the bulk supplies to break even on the transport. The thing is, the type of tourists that Nic was attracting don't really care too much about cost. If they like it that much they will pay, it's as simple as that, it reminds them of the vacation. And they do say the taste is unique."

Knowing rich people, having observed them in the old days, I could agree with his summary. "There is one question that has been bothering me," I said. "It's probably really silly but…"

"Go on then."

"Well there is so much topsoil here, how did you get it in through that airlock?"

Davis laughed, "You've got it wrong – the soil is crushed rock from Reevis; it's had organic matter mixed in with it, leaf mould and compostables from food waste amongst other things."

Davis drove me back to the hotel, where they told me that my stuff had arrived from the Splendid. I went up to my room; all my clothes had been pressed and hung in the walk-in wardrobe. I got a beer from the fridge and had a long soak in the bath, adding a packet of 'Genuine Reevis Mineral Salts' to the water; they were supposed to help with muscle aches and relax you. Another possible export, I thought drowsily as I lay in the steaming water.

I was so full of good food that I decided not to bother with a meal. The bath had made me feel sleepy so I stayed in the room and started writing my review. The video was still out from the solar wind and after a couple of pages I found it hard to stay awake. I gave up, set my alarm and went to sleep in the most comfortable bed I had used for ages.

12

Next morning I was in the lobby at six; the desk had called me just before my alarm went off and I had showered and had a coffee. I really felt refreshed from my sleep, a new experience to me, and I hadn't had any bad dreams. I reckoned I was ready to face an excursion outside the dome. I kept telling myself it was safe enough, but I remembered the leaking old prison transport and the fight for the masks as we plummeted down. Maybe I would be alright in the vehicle, as long as I didn't have to put a suit on and leave that. I was getting closer to vacuum – from the thickness of the hull of a liner to that of the dome, now the tour vehicle, I was getting better, one step at a time. My tame shrink had suggested that I couldn't be afraid of open spaces and enclosed spaces at the same time; she said that prison made you hate enclosed space and be frightened of open ones and if it came right down to it I would accept open, but I didn't necessarily agree. Maybe I would find out today.

Al turned up right on time, dressed as I was in overalls. After saying hello we walked down to the lounge. May was there in a boiler suit and was carrying a bag of tools. "May is one of our engineers; she's been checking the EV out."

"Everything is good, Al. Morning, Miles," she said cheerfully. "The cargo is loaded and it's all topped up, fuel, water and atmosphere. I've even put your lunch in the cool locker."

"Good girl," said Al, giving her a peck on the cheek, "we'll be back this afternoon." She nodded at me and went behind her desk, where she opened a cupboard full of boxes.

"She's checking spares. Come on then, Miles," said Al, "we'll stroll down to the bay."

We set off past the desk down a carpeted hallway with a gentle slope; there were signs everywhere in glowing lines of twisted neon. 'Wonders of the Worlds', 'See the Birth of the Planets', 'Safety Guaranteed', and many more. Large photographs lined the walls, the dome from the outside and the star peeking through gaps in the cliffs featuring heavily. As we descended underground, the carpet gave way to a concrete floor, the walls changed from wood panelling to riveted metal and the air took on a damp smell. The floor levelled out and I could see a light ahead.

"Are you feeling OK about this?" asked Al. "Only after yesterday I wouldn't want to rush you."

"No, it's fine," I replied, "I've managed to convince myself that it's pretty safe."

"That's good. You know, more people choke on peanuts in bars than die in space every year."

That made me grin and I thought of Flanagan. It took my mind off things a bit but the idea of being in a vehicle separated from the void by 20mm of metal and glass was still a bit worrying. A bit like the shuttle except that I would still be on solid ground.

Eventually we started walking uphill and arrived above ground. I realised we had walked about a mile through a tunnel in the cliffs and were now in a small isolated dome. As my eyes became accustomed, I could see stars through the Plastoglass. We were in a small gully in the shadow of the cliffs and it was pitch black, except for some blue lights on the frame of the dome. There was no sign of the other domes, or of anything manmade outside, except a yellow light that flashed rhythmically, not far outside the lock.

There was a line of four vehicles; all of them were multiwheeled and looked like large caterpillars. They were painted bright yellow with 'Al's Tours' in large black letters next to a number on the side. There was a line of ports down each side of the front sections; the rear had no windows and was probably where the propulsion and storage was housed. There was a line of floodlights on each roof with roll bars and heavy rubber fendering all over the hulls.

"They're methane powered," said Al, "we get the gas as a by-product from the oxygen separator in the power plant. Mix it with oxygen and it burns a treat."

Al ignored the first two, which were large, and headed for one of the smaller ones. "We'll take number one today," he explained, "the others take twelve passengers but these are only six plus two, plenty big enough for what we're doing."

I followed him and climbed onto a small platform on the back of the vehicle, then in through a sliding door into a small lock. It would have been a bit of a squeeze for the two of us in suits in vacuum, but the inner door was already open. We ducked into the cabin. Inside were two rows of seats, each by a port. They were luxuriously upholstered in what looked like leather and had small drinks tables on the arm by the port. The floor was hard vinyl. There were overhead lockers signed to contain suits and emergency gear.

More significantly there was a coffin draped in a flag resting across the seats on the right-hand side.

"Like I said," Al pointed, "I've got a reason to go up to the lookout today – last wishes and respect for an old mate."

Al had gone on ahead, past a curtain into the cockpit and as the door hissed shut behind me I had a sudden thought. I realised that even though I liked Al I hardly knew him or his views on anything, only that he had known Nic. All of yesterday's story could have been just that. He may even have been Nic's killer. And now I was completely at his mercy. The coffin could be just a prop, a disposal of evidence.

Al had settled into the pilot swivel chair on the right and

I took the one to his left. "Don't touch anything, please," he said and his hands danced over the controls as lights flashed.

"I wouldn't dream of it," I replied, as I watched the lights. Reds and ambers turned to greens and behind me there was a rumble from the power plant. The lights settled into a full set of greens that while reassuring meant little to me. They were so well laid out that a single red would be immediately apparent.

There was a large screen in the middle of the dashboard and it came on, showing a map of the crater with what I guessed was us as a flashing dot. There was a line of controls on one side of the screen and Al fiddled with them. The picture rotated and zoomed in, until it showed our dot in the dome, with a yellow dot in front of us.

"I won't bother you with all the safety stuff," said Al, "just do what I do if we have a problem, but we won't need it." It occurred to me that that was a strange thing to say; maybe I was in more danger here than I had realised. There was a jolt and it all became academic.

We started to move slowly towards a doorway that opened as we approached. We entered an airlock and the door slid shut behind us. Level with the port by Al's head was a display that showed the atmosphere decreasing as the lock voided.

"Are you okay?" asked Al, glancing across at me. "Only you're sweating."

"Sorry, as you know I'm not a big fan of vacuum, or being locked in." That was an understatement, but it was the best I could manage, my mouth was so dry that it sounded like a croak. I started hyperventilating, sucking air in huge gasps as I saw the numbers count back to zero. Al had a headset on and he called the control room: "Dome Control, this is Alpha Tango Zero One requesting permission to leave the dome on a tour."

A metallic voice came over the air, "Alpha Tango Zero

One you are so cleared, we have your details on mapping. Dome Control out."

"Don't worry," he said with a grin, "we're safe enough in here, it's all been checked out by May; we have suits and locators, auto return and a beacon." That was all very well but it would only take a few seconds for all the air to drain out, and I was sure that I couldn't get a suit on in that time. And could we trust May? I felt like I was getting paranoid.

I tried a nervous laugh. "Old story, I'll tell you later."

A buzzer sounded in the cab as the readout hit zero and the door in front of us opened. Ahead was nothing as we crawled forwards out of the lock, our lights making pools of white in the grey rock of the crater. We swung left towards the flashing yellow light until it was in front of us.

"That's the first marker post," said Al. "They're all linked to satellite and they show on the map." He pointed to the display screen in front of me where the dot had become a small outline of our craft, with numbers by the side. "That shows our direction, speed and the number on board," said Al. The model was moving slowly from left to right towards the yellow dot which I had taken to be a representation of the post. On the screen the post had numbers next to it, and I saw them on a sign attached to the post as we drove past. Another one was shown on the display ahead of us and as I looked up I could see its light. It was a different colour.

"Why is that one orange?" I asked.

"Junctions," replied Al. "They remind you to take care of mad men coming at you from the side." He laughed. "The posts mark the surveyed routes," Al continued, "and everyone keeps left of them; the ground is pretty flat in the crater, but there are a few holes here and there so we keep close to the line between the posts."

Other vehicles were visible on the display, which all had small arrows and the same set of numbers showing their direction and speed. "You can interrogate them to see more information, owners, what they're up to and their intended route," said Al. "If they get close, or if the tracking computer thinks they will, an alarm goes off. Any closer then Dome Control will get involved."

It all sounded well organised. "I guess there is some sort of distress alert?"

"Sure," he said. "You see this big button here," he pointed to a large red mushroom on the dashboard, under a plastic cover, "if you press it then we broadcast a different message and our model will flash red on everyone else's screens. Anyone close will respond, it's the unwritten law round here – you see a distress, you go to it."

There were areas on the map marked in red and I pointed to one. "They're prohibited to us, could be research or blasting or just unsurveyed," Al explained. "Dome Control watches everything out here and keeps everyone updated on traffic and hazards. They have a big radar set on the top of the cliffs. But they don't cover the entire crater; down to the south it's everyone for themselves."

We passed groups of suited figures, conducting drilling or other operations. Some of the rigs had the Balcom symbol on them, while some were plain. There were all sorts of vehicles, some stationary, some slower ones which we overtook, all with various bits of equipment on them. The large trailers had living units on them; I guessed they must be the ones that the farm supplied food to. One which featured quite heavily was like a crane, but the jib had a drill mounted on it; it was carried stowed flat, poking out like a lance, but in use was raised by hydraulics to the vertical. Another had a gun-like arrangement, again on a jib that Al told me fired explosive charges into the ground. All in all it was a hive of industry. The radio kept up a constant chatter, monitoring arrivals and departures, passing messages and issuing broadcasts. I kept hearing the word Doris and a number and asked Al about it.

"It's the drill rigs," he answered with a grin. "The official name is Drilling Rig Mark fifteen, so everyone calls them Doris. Look at the chart." I watched and we came up to one of the rigs; on the chart it said DR15 – I could see straight away what he meant. "So much easier than Delta Romeo One Five," he explained. "You have to keep it amusing or you'd go crazy."

"And what are we?" I asked, expecting to hear some weird name.

"We're an EV, that's Excursion Vehicle, but I'm passenger carrying so I've got a proper call-sign – the miners and cargo rigs are just Doris or Tug or Multi, for Multi-purpose – and a company ID number."

"It seems quite crowded out here," I said. There was a lot more traffic and activity than I had reckoned.

"There are a lot of prospectors, as well as the Corporation stuff," explained Al, "and some experimental work, stuff that needs a vacuum. It's quite rich pickings in the crater, bits of comet or meteor or whatever hit here, but as we go out it gets quieter. The far side of the crater is covered with ice. There's a road up in the cliffs which goes all round this side of the crater. You get a lot of traffic on it from the mines, ice and other stuff."

I realised that I had calmed down a bit. Maybe it was the awareness that if Al was going to kill me he would have been suited or we would both die together. Obviously I was safe for a while. Strangely, I was relaxing into the seat and felt comfortable being in this environment.

The plain was featureless, apart from the manmade things, up to the shadow of the cliffs. We seemed to be heading for the centre of the crater. "Didn't you say we were going up to the lookout?" I asked, trying not to sound worried.

"That's right," he agreed, "but first I thought that I'd take you to see the Ugly Sisters. It's a big landmark and part of the tour."

We were bouncing over the rough terrain; the independent suspension was coping pretty well with the uneven surface, which seemed to be mainly rock laid over with grey dust. The lights threw up reflections from sparkling crystals, probably silica although they could have been diamonds for all I knew. There was a line as straight as an arrow on the ground ahead of us, the ground past it was bathed in light. I could see the far wall of the crater, lit from halfway up.

"That's the sunrise," Al informed me. As we passed it the inside of the EV lit up, the ports darkened and polarised and bright rays shone in through the ports on our right-hand side. The next post had no light, but was coloured and twice as big. "They don't need lights this side of the shadow," Al said, "just a colour."

I had heard of the Ugly Sisters. In the middle of the crater was a column of rock, about eighty metres high. At some time in the past it had suffered a meteor strike which had split it in half, and from some angles the shape now resembled two people standing close together, arms raised as if arguing.

Looking at the map display, I could see it on the edge of the screen, and as we passed another of the orange posts Al turned left towards it. Our speed was quite fast, for some reason I had assumed that we would travel slowly. Maybe it was normal on the surveyed routes. We passed a green post. "That means we're off the controlled routes," Al forestalled my question, "there could be traffic from any direction here."

Sure enough as we closed on the twin columns of rock, in the light they really did look like two arguing people, the shadows behind them adding to the depth of the illusion. The ground was churned by multiple tracks. "That's mostly my tourist traffic," said Al. "The people working out here have seen them before; they have better things to do anyway."

We swung around the formation a couple of times, passing through its shadow and viewing it from every angle, then we headed back towards the green post, which could be seen in the distance. Looking back towards the domes, the star was visible above the cliffs, but with the polarised glass we could look directly as the parallax made it set. The cluster and the flashing lights past the line showed brightly against the dark cliffs but today no aura was visible. Again we passed the green post, then the orange one and then the black line and plunged back into semi darkness. Al swung the EV and we headed towards the cliffs, which quickly loomed over us.

13

As we dropped under the shadow of the cliffs even the rosy glow disappeared. Al turned on the light bar on top of the EV as we started to climb out of the crater, up a ramp that had clearly been manmade as it wove through columns of rock in a switchback fashion. I had visions of meeting traffic coming the other way on one of the blind corners – we weren't slowing down at all.

Al must have read my mind. "This is the up ramp," he said, "we don't have to worry about meeting anyone coming the other way; the down ramp is a lot shallower, with fewer corners."

We gained altitude quickly and soon could look down on the cluster of domes almost lost in the vast crater, just a collection of points of light. The temperature increased as did the light level, and the coolers came on inside the cabin.

As we levelled out on the crater rim, there was a broad roadway, at least fifty metres wide. Using the natural features it had been carved out of the rock, which had been compressed by a myriad of overlapping tyre tracks and the centre line was dotted with more of the marker posts. Where there were gaps in the cliffs there were sheer drops on both sides, with no safety railings. Patchy bright sunlight illuminated the road through gaps on the hot side, flickering as we sped past. Where the cliffs were solid, deep shadows hid the road. We passed over a bridge, crossing a deep chasm. "This is incredible," I said to Al. "How long did this take to make?"

"Not long," he answered with the complacent air of one who has done much harder jobs. "We just got a couple of big munchers in, levelled it and built the ramps in no time. The bridge was assembled in orbit and flown into place. There's a few dotted around."

There was a lot of traffic, drilling rigs, and large loaders filled with rock or ice; most of them flashed their lights at us as we passed them, and I noticed that Al did the same. The larger or slower ones going the same way kept over to the edge so we could pass. Radio traffic was constant.

"Most of this is Balcom traffic," he said. "They have research stations and mines dotted along the crater rim and further out on the ice. They used to give me grief, but now they generally get out of the way. I saved one of their drivers a while ago and I think it dawned on them that if they carried on bugging me, I might not bother again."

It was a familiar story: the overriding enemy was the environment, just as Harris had said in his journal, and everything else was secondary. And it didn't matter if the man coming the other way was your enemy; he might just be around to save your life.

We rode along until we came to a larger gap in the cliffs, on the hot side. Al slowed as we came level with the gap, letting the traffic clear, then swung the wheel and we turned down what proved to be a wide canyon, twisting through the wall of the crater rim. The shape of it stopped light coming through, but I noticed that it was lit by floodlights on the walls. "Solar panels on the outside of the cliffs," explained Al.

The high walls of grey rock flashed past, eventually becoming a tunnel as we headed towards the hot side.

"This is my lookout. It's an observation position I set up, and it's the best part of my tours." The cave meandered a bit, gradually getting brighter, until we turned into a large opening. The cave had been blocked off with the familiar hexagonal framed Plastoglass; there was an airlock big enough for the larger EVs. We fitted in easily. When the door closed behind us, Al called the Dome Control and closed down. He told them we were performing a funeral and would be a few hours.

"Call us again before you depart," they advised.

Meanwhile the lock had pressurised and we drove into the lookout.

14

It was a space about thirty metres across, with a Plastoglass wall at the outside edge, through which the sun shone. I couldn't see the star from my position and was just about to move closer when Al distracted me. "Leave that for a minute and look at this," he called as he went to a small door in the cliff, close to the join between the glass and the rock.

"This is the utility space," he said. "We've got a small oxygen generator in here, every month or so you fill it with ice and it separates it out. Methane and oxygen is stored so we can refuel the EV up here. The climate control is all automatic. Back there we've used the tunnel, enlarging it to make space for a kitchen, bunks and all the facilities. Before we bring the tourists up here, the caterers come and set up for lunch. We turn this part into a dining room. We have lunch looking at that."

He pointed to the glass wall and I moved forward as he pulled hoses from the room and attached them to the EV.

The Plastoglass wall in front of us was polarised and tinted, so that I could see the star and the havoc on the molten sea below.

The star shone brightly down at about thirty degrees elevation, and it felt strange to know that it was always in the same place, watching the convulsions of the planet. As far as the eye could see, lava flowed like water, boiling and bubbling under the immense forces generated by the star's continual radiation, it washed around outcrops of the denser rocks, stranded like islands in the molten ocean. It crashed against the cliffs below us in explosions of superheated surf, throwing up spray which cooled and rattled against the glass like hailstones.

The display was made all the more impressive by the lack of sound; of course there was no atmosphere for the sound waves to travel in.

I could have stood and watched it forever, so hypnotic was the sight. Obviously the Plastoglass was specially designed to take the continual battering. I touched it and it felt cool. Looking past my hand I thought I saw movement out on the bubbling lava. I looked again and there was definitely a craft floating out there. It was built like a submarine, with aerials on the top and it drifted around with the currents, glowing in the heat. Who would want to be out there?

"What the hell is that?" I called to Al. "Have you seen this?" He crossed to the glass and followed my finger.

"Oh that's a skimmer," he said in a bored voice. "They suck up all the lighter elements that float on top of the lava."

"But how do they survive?"

They float on a cushion of supercooled plasma," he answered. "The bulk of the thing are the generators for the two Tokamak sets, one at each end. In the middle is a suction hose and all the filtering gear. It's made of composite. Balcom have a high-tech facility over on the cold side making heat-resistant polymers and ceramics."

I stood and watched, in awe. "Isn't it risky for the pilots?"

"Sure," said Al, "but the value of the skim is so high that the company can afford to lose one every now and again. Anyway the pilots are in a pod, with its own life support and engines. Any problems and they have an auto eject. The pay's pretty good as well, which means there are plenty of volunteers." I was once again in awe of mankind's efforts to use the things that they found on their travels in space.

"You think that this is spectacular," he said, "I have another place like this, on the cold side, with a scenic drive through the ice fields, all lit by floodlights; there are amazing shadows and ice formations. It's just as magnificent in its own way." It was said with pride. "Mind you this one is the most popular. Sorry to disturb you but we have a job to do."

Between us, respectfully, we lifted Nic's coffin onto a trolley that Al had removed from the utility locker and brought around to the EV's door. We wheeled it over to a small airlock in the side of the glass frame, over a smooth stone ramp, rather like a ski-jump. The inner door shut with a clunk and Al cast his eyes down.

"Goodbye, old friend," he said. "I'm not one for words at a time like this, but I'll miss you, and I won't rest until I get closure, till I find out who and why and finish what you started."

Simple words powerfully said, and sentiments that I could understand.

He pushed a button and the outer door slid to one side. The coffin tipped up and slid down the slope, picking up speed until it soared into the heaving lava with a soundless ripple. The door closed and Al turned to me. He looked like he was about to cry. I spoke to break the moment.

"Do you do a lot of funerals up here?"

"You might be surprised; it was part of the reason that I was able to get the money together to build this place. But that's enough small talk," he said. "Now that I have your undivided attention, tell me about Nic. What happened?"

He didn't have my undivided attention, not by a long way, but tearing my thoughts away from the spectacle, I told him what I knew: about finding Nic's body, the police and the turning over of my room. I didn't mention the drive, or all of Flanagan's comments. Al listened without batting an eye until I described Nic's body, wedged in the bathroom blocking the door as it tried to open. It sounded like so undignified an end that, as I paused for breath, Al turned his face away from me, shoulders shaking.

I realised then that he could not have been involved and that I was quite safe – the show of emotion was too real to be an act. Before I knew it I had blurted out my concerns about the police's involvement in events, and he became serious again.

"Miles," said Al, "I've decided to give you the full story. You've heard the factions, they all have a bit of the whole, but Nic and I were among the few who've managed to piece it all together. It's the real reason Nic wanted you here. Get comfortable because I'm going to tell it for him."

I sat down in one of the leather chairs facing the lava and Al sat opposite, with his back to the show. He thought for a moment and then began.

15

"What I'm going to tell you started about three years ago, with a safety inspection that revealed faults in the monitoring system on the outer dome. You know there is a net?"

I nodded and he continued, "and you know any meteor strike is detected and a crew sent to investigate. Well on one inspection they found that a small meteor had hit the control box for the sensors. A real freak shot. It's only half a metre across. But instead of an alarm, somehow it had jammed the system open, so the computer thought everything was normal. So there had been a large section of dome with no monitoring for oxygen leakage or rock strike for quite a while. And there were some minor problems that had not been fixed early, so it cost more to repair in the end."

"With you so far," I said, wondering where this was leading.

"Well the new Balcom manager, Tony Hays, had reduced the maintenance budget and inspection frequency. That's why the fault went unnoticed for so long. The general view was that the money he had saved was going into his own pocket, but that's just a guess. Realising that the whole dome had been unsafe for who knows how long made him unpopular with the old hands, people like Harris Morgan and Nic, who saw it as penny pinching and asking for trouble. After all, it wasn't just the dome; it was the whole colony that was at stake. But Donna Markes, the new Vice President of Balcom, had appointed him so nothing changed. And his wife is Donna Markes's sister as well, which is probably how he got the job. In the end Harris toed the line and Nic got fired."

It looked like this was turning into another tale of corporate mismanagement.

Al continued, "Anyone that tried to raise the issue was told to shut up. Tony was out to make a name for himself by saving money. He figured that with his family connections he could maybe get a top job – he was a graduate, what did these uncouth engineers know, with their dirty fingernails. It seemed like he could do what he wanted."

While he was talking Al had got up and was setting up the large table in the corner, ready for our lunch.

"He had had a lucky escape with the dome, but it made people start to take more notice of his actions. Pretty soon a whole lot of dubious practices were spotted. Stories spread and he was always denying them. The gossip was getting out of hand. Almost overnight, restrictions were put on travel off-planet for the workforce and their families, the comms satellite was monitored and censored, dissenters found themselves shunted sideways and people like Nic found themselves out of a job."

So it was the usual self-preservation story of corrupt leaders everywhere.

"Tony brought in a lot of new people who could control the workforce and the spread of information. His wife – Shelly is her name, real bitch – anyway, she set up a sort of private security service, spying on people they thought might cause trouble."

"Shelly!" I exclaimed. "Dark hair, blue eyes, tall."

"That's her," he agreed.

"I met her in the main dome; she told me she was Harris Morgan's daughter."

He laughed. "That sounds like her, she can't talk without lying, and she was probably trying to get you to say something inappropriate. Mind you, she and Harris are two of a kind so maybe she is."

"Well I didn't satisfy her on the inappropriate bit." I didn't mention the look I had seen in her eyes.

"Well done. If you had have, you'd be drilling holes alone on the cold side."

That was a sobering thought, but marginally better than lying in a hotel bathroom. I told him that the Rangers had said that I was being followed.

"They're a smart bunch. Tony and Shelly hate them, any Balcom workers whose kids so much as look at the Rangers are warned off."

Al took a drink and continued, "A small, private company had just finished building the farm dome, independent from Balcom; they had a government subsidy to encourage the growth of the settlement, and a backup dome, something that Balcom now didn't want. Because I was already here they hired me to set up the ecosystem and I stayed on to manage it for them, although I'm doing less now as Davis has started to take over. The farm had its own power station and that gave them some measure of independence. I helped Nic get himself a job and he moved over here. Tony Hays now had his scapegoat, someone he could blame for anything. And because he had sacked so many people, the Balcom farm couldn't compete. Tony had to shut it down and contract with the new farm, which made him hate us even more."

"It sounds to me like he's in over his head; everything he does to cover up makes it worse. He would have made a great politician." I hadn't realised the farm was nominally independent; I must admit I had thought it was all federal or Balcom.

"Oh he's a very clever man, and he has the support of Donna Markes. So things have got worse. Tony Hays gets worried that the Balcom people will tell their story to non-Balcom staff, and word will get out. So Shelly and Tony discourage fraternisation, and the easiest way is to demonise off-worlders, or anyone who isn't Balcom. He has to keep restrictions on movement, so to justify it he comes up with the industrial espionage story, and the overpopulation line is used as well – all tools to keep a secret. He's become paranoid about the government getting wind of what's really going on here. There would be inspectors crawling all over the place, and whatever else Balcom was up to would get out. There are a lot of important research projects based here, but the government lets Balcom run them and they tell the government only what they want them to hear. You'd be surprised just how easy it is to control a planet, especially if you have the resources of Balcom to spin the news and bury the bad stuff."

I was trying to take this all in. "So how did I get here?"

"Well, when you tell it all at once it sounds like a big thing, but it developed over a year or so, a little bit at a time. Mostly it's just minor inconvenience – the comms go down, or someone gets pushed sideways. Customs are really thorough outwards and a lot of people are refused travel if they're on 'sensitive' work. No one really sees the big picture, unless they are quite senior. And you never know who you're talking to; it could be one of Shelly's men. So people shrug and keep to themselves. Anyone they don't know is a possible threat. It's very clever psychology, divide and rule. As long as you don't poke about in Balcom business, or attract their attention, you can do what you like."

I thought about the drive I had posted to Gaynor – would it get off world? At least I still had the original. I could put it in my press bag when I left, officially it was exempt from customs search. But maybe I should keep my head down a little.

Al carried on, "The police in general try to keep a lid on things. The Mayor is in Balcom's pocket and certainly on the inside. There are some honest officials, it's just hard to know which ones."

What he had just told me fitted in with the bits and pieces I had found out for myself. It all sounded plausible, and my purpose here was obviously more than I had thought. But if I was to bring the whole edifice down I needed more than just talk.

16

The EV had been stocked with a gourmet lunch, and we enjoyed a two person wake whilst gazing at the lava field. "Sorry, no alcohol today," Al explained when I mentioned that a glass of wine would complement the meal. "We do for tourists but I'm driving and you are my co-pilot."

I looked worried – I couldn't drive the EV.

Al laughed. "Relax, it's a courtesy title, but there's only two of us so no booze. We'll be off soon and we'll head straight back; the down ramp is a lot closer to the cluster than the one we came up."

We packed up and Al disconnected the hoses from the EV. "We're full of fuel and air," he said. "We had plenty but it never hurts to top up. We do need ice in the converter, I'll have to remind May to get it organised." He checked the control panel and downloaded something to a drive-store. "That's the system log since I was last here. Right, the alarms are all set, we can go now."

While we were in the airlock, Al called in our departure details and the controller advised that there was a convoy of ore carriers heading inward to the cluster on our route. Al acknowledged and turned to me. "Apart from them, it won't be too busy on the way back, so we shouldn't get held up too much on the ramp. There are plenty of passing places."

We backed out of the airlock, then Al turned the EV in the tunnel where a wide depression had been carved out of the rock; the wheels on each side of the EV could be driven independently so it turned in a very small space. The computer controlled the traction; there was a wheel for steering and two pedals, the selectors for forward or reverse gearing and the brakes were on the wheel itself.

"Do you want to drive?" Al asked me after we were facing the right way. I'll turn on the dual controls – if I don't like what you're up to I'll take over." Put like that I could hardly refuse, and I could drive a car so what could be so different? He extended the wheel in front of me and showed me two buttons on the inside of the handgrips. "Put your fingers over them. Each one brakes that side's wheels, the pedals are the accelerators. The direction switches are by your thumbs. Just take it slow down the canyon till you get the hang of it."

The wheel was well designed and touching the buttons felt natural. I pushed both thumb switches forward; there was a whine of hydraulics. "That's it," said Al, "now gently on the pedals. If you want to stop, fingers on the brakes."

I pressed both pedals and we started to move. Turning the wheel brought an instant response but I could have been on a simulator, there was no feel for the road conditions. My confidence increased as the canyon widened a little so I gave it what I thought would be a little bit more speed. We leapt away and in a panic I pressed the brakes. Instantly we stopped with a jolt, dust billowing from our wheels as they locked in a skid that took us toward the rocks. The engine shut off and everything was quiet.

My hands shaking, I turned to Al, who was doubled up with laughter. "The look on your face. I should have mentioned the pedals are not linear, power increases exponentially as you press them down. Never mind, have another go."

"Are you crazy?" I exclaimed. "I nearly ran us into that rock – the hull would have gone and that would have been us."

His face turned serious. "No it wouldn't, the computer would have sensed the rock and taken control. Even if we had hit it, the fendering would have absorbed the impact. You're safe in here, these are pretty tough. A drill or an explosive charge might crack the hull, but anything while we're in motion won't cause us a problem."

"I don't think I'll have another go, just at the moment," I told him and he nodded.

"Fair enough." He left my wheel out and restarted the engine.

We got back to the roadway and were just about to emerge from the canyon when a large lorry shot past the entrance at high speed. It had a drill rig on the back and several trailers of gear. It was followed by a stream of ore carriers and it took us several minutes before we could join the road. Al looked pleased. "That'll be the convoy. Now they won't be breathing down our necks all the way back, trying to get past."

Did he really think that I could cope with that amount of traffic, in a strange vehicle on this road?

"That's why I let you drive, back there," he said. "I've been watching them on the map and I figured that if we let you have a slow practice in the canyon they would be past us by the time you got here. Then you would have an open road all the way back."

"Oh go on then, let me have another go." I put my hands on the wheel and pressed the pedals.

After a few minutes on this wide open road I felt almost at home driving the EV. I even started glancing down at the map. Al sat back beside me, hands behind his head, totally relaxed. I even started to hum a tune to myself. The flickering from the sunshine through the gaps in the cliffs had a hypnotic effect and I started thinking about my life.

The open view across the crater was making me wish I didn't live in the middle of a huge clump of humanity. I had always enjoyed open spaces, hence the yacht, and since my imprisonment I longed for a far horizon with nothing in the way. I realised that I could live here. If only the people didn't seem so intent on screwing it up, this place could be a paradise.

111

And it would be nice to find someone to share it with.

"Miles," Al's voice brought me back to the present. I realised that I had been driving for a long while without thinking about what I was doing. I must have been getting the hang of it. "We're coming to the down ramp – do you want me to take over?"

I felt confident. "No, if you're happy I'll carry on for a bit."

He grinned. "Got you hooked. OK the ramp is shallow, so the heavy transports don't run away, and the corners are wide. Just keep the speed down and the governors on the axles will help to adjust the braking."

We came around the last corner before the ramp and there was a large rig in front of us. I had seen it on the map but didn't know how to find its speed. "How do I get the information on that rig?" I asked Al.

"I'll do it," he replied, "you worry about the driving."

He fiddled around for a while as the rig got closer. I eased the pedals and we slowed down behind it. I had got the hang of juggling the pedals and the brakes, our motion smooth.

"It's alright," he announced, "they're heading straight on. Just stay behind them, you're doing great." His words gave me confidence as we crawled along behind the enormous trailer.

As we neared the top of the ramp, the rig in front of us accelerated away, leaving us alone.

That's strange, I thought, why suddenly do that? There was a sign in the rock: DOWN RAMP 200M RIGHT.

"Nothing coming," said Al, "just swing onto it as we pass the post."

The flashing orange post dropped behind us and I could see the wide entrance to the ramp. I turned into it and set-tled in the middle of the gap; there were cliffs on one side and a drop on the other.

I could see what he meant. The straights were long and gave a view over the crater; each turn was slow and gentle. The levelled way was a lot wider, so that the slower loads would not hold up traffic. As we descended, the natural light quickly dimmed and Al turned on more of the EV's lights. They created shadows on our left side that followed us down.

To our right, the crater lay spread out before us, the cluster providing a splash of colour, and the unmoving line of shadow showed the sunrise. In the distance the Ugly Sisters stood out even more, lit from halfway up. Random lights moved around the crater, marking the surveyors and other rigs. It all looked very welcoming. Around it and spread out were the flashing lights of the marker beacons and individual pinpoints showing traffic. I started to feel relaxed; just a short while and I would be soaking in a warm bath of mineral salts, followed by a couple of beers. The sights I had seen today had made me even surer that Nic had been on the right track, this place could be a destination to rival any. It just needed to sort the locals out. I could see in my mind the potential, just like he had.

We swung around the next turn. It had been built around a pillar of rock, and as we came out of it the map alarm went off, jerking me out of my dreams. It showed a vehicle ahead of us which appeared to be descending slowly as we caught it up.

Al pressed buttons. "Ore carrier. It'll be going slow, with all the weight."

I asked Al if we would overtake it. "Depends on the width," he answered, "there's room on some of the straights and we'll see when we get closer." We came around another corner and saw the other rig, but it wasn't going down slowly at all.

It was stopped – no it was coming straight for us. And it was wide. One side of it was hard up against the rock face, leaving a gap on the edge.

17

Al swore and grabbed his wheel. "Let go," he shouted and I gladly gave him control. We swung across the road, headed straight towards the drop. At the last minute he turned away from it, the computer juggling the traction controls to speed the turn. I could feel the wheels bite into the surface, gravel and dust flying up around the cab. Now we had a clear run down the side of the road but now that the rig had got us on that side it was cutting across the roadway and the gap grew smaller. They had pushed us to take the outside, and now they were forcing us over. Al accelerated as I saw the gap get smaller.

It was all very tight, but maybe we would get past. The edge loomed, with a vertical drop and boulder-filled patches about fifty metres below. Another alarm blared and Al took his hands off the steering. "Auto has taken control," he said and we watched, helpless as the distance decreased.

Whoever was in control of the other machine had a clear purpose: kill us both. We were right on the edge of the roadway, the drop sucking at us and still it came. Our outer wheels went over the edge and we slid sideways. The rig loomed large, filling the ports on my side as gravity took control and we slid sideways, tipping over and away from it. I realised that the windscreen of the rig was obscured, so the driver was invisible as it passed. Then I saw stars as we flipped.

We rotated in the air and slammed into the ground, knocking us dizzy. The roll bars and fendering on the roof cushioned our impact, but even so I felt the wind knocked out of me. The lights went out and all the loose objects in the cabin bounced off the hull and into our heads. Pieces of paper, coffee cups, fluff and all manner of things rained down on us, and the darkness made it more terrifying. There were some heavier objects bouncing around as well, one of them must have hit Al as he shouted out. At least the coffin was gone – being assaulted by a corpse in the dark would have been unimaginably frightening.

The EV bounced and landed upright on its wheels at the edge of another drop. Amazingly the pressure hull had stood up to the impact, and we could still breathe. Although we rocked as we balanced on the lip of the drop our wheels still turned. The automation shut down the power, and despite the alarms that still sounded it suddenly felt peaceful. Blue emergency lighting came on. I could hear muffled cursing from Al somewhere behind me; he could not have been strapped in and lay on the side of the hull. I turned my head and could see him, wedged between the seats. His face was covered in blood, but he smiled weakly at me.

"Perhaps I should have done the safety briefing after all," he croaked.

"Are you badly hurt?" I asked him. My head was swimming and my ribs felt sore with every breath, probably from the seatbelt strap.

"I don't think so," he answered. "I can move my arms and legs but I've cut my head. Something must have hit it." He raised his hand and wiped at his forehead. "It's only a small cut but it's bleeding a lot. There's a first aid box under my seat, I need a dressing."

I leant over towards his seat but the movement sent the EV rocking on the lip. It slid sideways about a foot and stopped. Looking out of the ports on the right showed a drop of twenty metres or so, over boulders and loose gravel to the edge of the roadway.

"Don't move any more," he called. "We're balanced on the lip, hang on a minute."

"How do I shut the alarms off?"

"Wait, I'm thinking." There was a scuffling noise behind me and we rocked a bit, but didn't slide any more. "I'm working my weight over to the high side," he said. "Can you lean up against the bulkhead?"

I transferred my position, undoing my belt, and lifted myself to sit on the seat arm.

That and Al's movement were enough to set the wheels on my side down on solid ground. Now Al appeared over my shoulder; reaching over me he pointed.

"Push that button," he said and I followed his finger. "Now lift the lever down by your left knee." There was a thud of compressed gas and a whine. Instantly the EV felt more secure. Al let out a sigh. "Ground anchors," he said, "fired by gas into the rock and self-tensioning. We won't go over now." He retreated and came round my seat into his, cancelling the alarms one by one.

We sat there for a moment, looking at each other. I reached under his seat again and found the first aid box. Al took it from me and opened a dressing pack. He pressed it to the side of his head. "That's better, let's sort ourselves out." His speech was a bit slurred and he seemed slightly disorientated.

He punched at controls and looked at screens; some were out but he managed to get them back. "Well do you want the good news or the bad?" he said after a couple of minutes. "Let's have the good first," I answered.

"OK," he said, "we're alive and the hull is intact, there appears to be no major axle damage and the power plant and tanks are secure. But, unless we can get more wheels on solid ground we're stuck here."

It could be worse then. "And the bad news?"

"Well the aerials are damaged, or maybe the transmitter, so we can't send a distress, plus the mapping is off so I can't see if there's anyone else around."

"What does that mean?" I asked, but I think I already knew the answer.

"We're walking out – get suited."

18

I felt a sudden surge of panic as I tried to think for a reason not to leave what felt like the safety of the EV. "What about the people who ran us off the road, might they be waiting for us?"

"Well we can't stop here," he replied, frowning with the effort of forming his words. "We have oxygen for about twelve hours but we can't be seen from the road. We can't send a distress, the mapping is offline so I can't tell if they've gone or not."

"Can't we use the anchors to lower us down or winch us sideways onto the rock?"

He thought for a moment. "Not really, the cables might not hold, anyway we can't drive from here to the road, it's too rocky."

All my fears were surfacing at once, my fear of suits and vacuum that I had overcome up to now. I had felt safe in the technology, now I could see a raw side to the place.

"I don't fancy walking," I said, unashamed to admit it.

"Neither do I," he answered, surprising me a little; I had thought him to be at home. "I hate the idea of walking but there really is no option. The first rule around here is stay with your vehicle. But that assumes that someone will be looking for you. We're out of sight here and haven't sent a distress, so we must attract attention somehow. We can probably drop to the next road and flag someone down. I don't expect we'll have to walk all the way back, but even if we did, it would only be about five hours."

I persisted, "Sounds good in theory, but they may be waiting for us to do just that."

He became exasperated. "Look if they had wanted to make sure they could have fired a drilling charge at us, which would have cracked the hull open and that would have been it. We can't just sit here."

Of course they might have been getting ready to do that right now, we just didn't know. "OK," I answered, resigned to it, "where are the suits?"

"Before we go," he said, "we eat until we can't eat any more, have a hot drink and then we go to the toilet. We can carry extra oxygen with us but nothing else."

He rummaged around in the back, bringing self-heating coffee cups and ration packs. It felt very much like the condemned man having his last meal and my stomach was cramped up with the thoughts of what lay ahead, plus I was still full from lunch. But I tried to follow his advice.

We finished our meal and used the facilities, then started to get suited. The food and coffee seemed to have revived Al and he was more like his usual self. He helped me fit into the suit, which was easier than I expected, and was showing me how to check the seals when there was a noise echoing through the EV. We stopped, tense and waiting for something else to happen. "Get the rest of your suit on, and the helmet, quickly," said Al, trying to sound calm for my benefit. I fumbled with the neck seal, the action made more difficult by the suit gloves. How did people live like this?

Rocks bounced on the roof. "What's that, Al?" I shouted.

"It's probably the stuff we loosened on our way down," was his reply. The noise came again, and then there was a rhythmic tapping on the hull. We stopped wrestling with our suits and looked at each other – someone was definitely outside.

The noise came again, tap tap tap on the rear door. Al turned the camera on; there was a suited figure on the screen waving a metal bar.

They were pointing to the side of their helmet, where the wearer's ears were, and then to our EV.

"They're trying to tell us to communicate," he said. It was a logical assumption.

I pulled a stylus from my pocket and grabbed a piece of paper from the debris on the deck. 'No radio, airtight, two of us' I wrote and went to the rear. Entering the lock I held it up against the port in front of the helmeted figure. The faceplate of the helmet was blank, but it nodded to show that it had read and understood. It turned and moved away.

I came back to Al. "What happened?" he asked.

"They've gone. Now we have to see whose side they are on when they come back."

After ten of the longest minutes of my life so far the figure returned and came round to the windscreen; they held up a black box. "That's an ultrasonic transceiver," Al told me. "It will pick up our conversation through the hull." He put his thumb up and the helmet nodded and moved away. There was a clang by the hatch, then a voice, tinny and distorted but unmistakably female.

"Hi, Al, are you having a spot of bother?" The understatement was breathtaking.

"Hiya," replied Al. "We're anchored and airtight, but could do with a lift out."

"Who's that?" I asked him, wondering just what the chances were of meeting someone he knew out here, stuck like this.

"It's Tash. She's a freelance explorer, she finds quite a bit of good stuff. She lives on her own out here for months, prospecting. I haven't seen her for ages. She's more Nic's friend than mine, nice lady though."

"Well you're in luck," Tash said, "I've got my mining rig up on the ramp above you. I'll bed it in and drop a line round your rear tow point. Probably easier to lower you down to the flat, it's a bit lumpy above you. Don't worry, you'll be sorted in no time. Bet your passenger wasn't expecting this."

"Too right," I said.

Her brisk manner inspired confidence and she kept up a constant chatter on the radio, telling us what she was doing as she stabilized her rig and set up its crane. There was a bit of a wait while she ran off some wire and rigged a block, hammering fixings into the rock, then she climbed back down and attached a hook to our rear tow point. We watched her work via the EV's camera, which Al could swivel on its mounting over the rear hatch. She performed the operation with an easy familiarity that inspired confidence. I was fairly practical myself when I needed to be but living out on her own meant that she had to be good at this sort of thing.

"Right," she said at last, "I've set up a snatch block on the rocks to give me a good lead on the wire. I'll take the weight and pivot you so that you're nose down. Start up and get ready for my instructions." Al settled himself at the controls and the engine rumbled into life.

Tash stayed by us with a large torch and a remote control for her crane and winch. She took the slack out of the wire and I felt us move slightly, the hull grating on the rock. It set my teeth on edge and I shuddered.

"Don't worry about that," Al told me seeing my face, "the floorpan is reinforced and there's nothing vital down there."

She took more of the weight of the EV on her winch and we released the ground anchors. She applied tension to the wire and the EV pivoted as she had planned. As more wheels came back into contact with the slope, Al applied power gently to the axles, taking some of the strain off of the wire. "Ease off," Tash instructed, "and I'll start to lower you down slowly."

Al cut the power and we tipped over the edge that we had been resting on. "I'm going to do this quickly," she called, and we dropped like a stone towards the ground. Our wheels bumped on the rock face and the ground rose up towards us, grey boulders and gravel in deep shadow. We had no lights so it was difficult to judge the distance we had to go. Suddenly we got stuck on an outcrop.

"Tash, stop! We're stuck," Al shouted.

"Hang on," she replied and the bright beam from her torch swept over us.

"OK I can see the problem," she said. "I'll haul you back up a bit." We rose, jerking back towards Tash. "Al, lock the steering hard right and put forward traction on the wheels." He did that and we crabbed sideways with Tash letting out the wire; this manoeuvre took us past the obstruction and we continued our descent.

Eventually we reached the slope by the roadway. The nose touched first and the fendering cushioned the impact. Al put power on the front wheels and they gripped in the loose gravel, moving us forward until we were level on the surface.

"Disconnect the wire," called Tash and Al opened the tow hook.

We thanked her, although it seemed inadequate. "I'll stow all my gear and tow you in if you wait a while," she said.

"Everything is looking fine here, except the comms," said Al. "We can manage but thanks."

"No sweat," she replied, "I'll tell Dome Control you're on the way in with no radio. See you again."

I thought that sounded a bit rude, after all she had done, so I had an idea. "I'll be in the hotel later," I said. "If you turn up I'd love to buy you a drink."

"Sounds good to me," she replied. "Who are you though?"

"That's Miles," Al said. "He thought he was just getting the standard tour."

Tash laughed. "I might just take you up on that, Miles. Now if you're sure you're OK I'll go and sort my rig out. See you later."

Al started down the road, I let him drive. We kept the speed down as we had no lights and every time we saw another vehicle we got over to the cliff side well out of their way. "Lucky it was someone you know," I said to Al.

"It wouldn't have mattered," he replied. "Everyone helps out here, cos you never know when you might need it. Like I said before, even if you don't get on, you don't turn away."

"Yes but this Tash had all the gear on her rig."

"Well that was lucky," he agreed, "but anyone else who found us would have called Dome Control and they would have sent someone with a crane, we would just have had to wait a little longer that's all."

I understood that but still couldn't handle the fact that someone had tried to kill us. All the time we were trying to survive it had gone to the back of my mind, now in comparative safety it resurfaced. "Someone tried to kill me," I said, "and I'm not used to that. Who do you think it was?"

"It may be the same ones who killed Nic," offered Al, "although they may have just been after me for something and you're just incidental."

That was the problem: we were both candidates for extinction. I was connected to Nic's death and had been followed since I had got here. Al was unpopular with Balcom and had survived threats before. It seemed that nobody wanted either of us around, and the more I had learned the more obvious it became that here was a major problem on Reevis.

The EV ran sweetly, a testament to its strong construction and we were soon off the ramp and on the crater floor, heading back to Al's base. Before we had gone very far, a small Tug came towards us with flashing lights and made us stop. We went through the rigmarole of setting up communications again; a lot easier as Tash had left the transceiver on our hull. As it only had a short range and Dome Control had been unable to call us they had sent the Tug looking.

"Let me do the talking," said Al, and explained that we had lost control and slipped over the edge of the down ramp, neglecting to give too much detail. After a short wait they offered to escort us back to Al's base. They peeled off as we entered the lock. "I'll have to write a report. I don't want to stir up trouble accusing anyone and we have no proof so I might have to say you were driving and blame you," he said. "Sorry in advance." I nodded in understanding as the lock pressurised.

When we got through the lock, Al parked the EV and as we walked back up the tunnel May came running down the corridor. Her face was pale and her mascara had run from crying. She threw herself into his arms and held him close.

"Al," she said between sobs, "are you alright? Tash called and said she had rescued you." Her devotion was touching and I felt lonelier than I had for a long time. She let go of Al and turned to me. "Excuse me, Mr Goram, I hope you're alright."

"Yes, I am, thanks to Al; he's a pretty special guy."

She looked at him adoringly. "He is to me."

"Tash was brilliant," Al said. "It was lucky she was around."

"She told me that she was coming in to see someone and heard you call from the lookout. She was catching you up when you vanished from the mapping. Come on, we're going for a drink," May announced, dragging Al by the arm. "Miles, won't you join us?"

I didn't want to intrude on their happiness so I thanked them and declined. I took the lift to my room and had a bath, soaking my aching ribs in more of the mineral salts. They were red and I suspected would be black and blue by the morning. But the salts helped and I could feel the muscles relax as I soaked. When the water cooled, I got out and put a towelling gown on.

I got my tablet out to carry on with my review. When I turned it on I saw that I had a new message; it was from Gaynor. 'Got your package, when are you coming back? Be safe, xxx'. That was a relief – my copy of Nic's drive had made it to Centra. I tried to concentrate on writing a bit more. But every time I closed my eyes I could see the rig coming towards us.

There was a knock at my door and I stopped typing. Looking out of the spyhole I could see a girl with dark hair.

"Who is it?" I called.

"I saved your life today, and you offered me a beer. May said you were up here." I opened the door.

19

She flowed into the room, lighting it up with her smile and the force of her personality. Her dark eyes swept over me, a faint grin on her face. "Hi, I'm Tash Perdue." She stuck out a hand and I shook it. It was a firm grip, a working person's grip. At her touch I felt my heart lurch, as if I had been plugged into the mains.

"I was coming back from the north edge when you dropped off the map. Then I saw you balanced halfway down – how did you end up there?"

She was tall, slim and brown-eyed, and with her dark hair coiled on top of her head it made her look even taller. She wore a dark boiler suit, which had been altered to fit closely, and dark boots. The effect was set off by a flash of white shirt at her throat and a silver belt. She looked like a top model in pristine working gear.

"We were run off the road; there was a rig coming up the down ramp."

She nodded, frowning. "I'll bet they had no ID on the map reader."

"Got it in one," I confirmed. "Does this happen a lot?"

She smiled. "That'll be a Balcom rig, it's typical of them. They don't like Al, although they normally just leave it at verbal abuse. I can't see them meaning to kill him though, frighten him maybe." She changed the subject. "You must be Nic's hotel guy; May said that you were."

She clearly didn't know that Nic was dead; it looked like everyone had left it for me to be the one to tell her.

"Well I'm glad you were about," I said. "At least someone was on our side. What's your story?"

She raised an eyebrow. "No hanging around with you is there, straight into journalist mode. OK, I'll play along, but it's thirsty work and you did promise me a beer."

"I'm sorry, hang on a minute, I'll get dressed," I said, aware of the fact that I was naked under the robe and feeling a little rude. Was I that out of practice with women? It had been a while but I should have behaved better. After all, she had saved my life so I should make more of an effort. It didn't seem to bother her.

"I can find them while you make yourself decent," she said, walking to the fridge. I ducked back into the bathroom and got dressed; when I emerged she was holding two bottles. She passed one to me and I felt that tingle again as our hands touched. We popped the caps and drank.

She went to sit on the couch in front of the picture window, tucking her legs up under her body. The aurora played around behind her head; it gave her an ethereal look. She took the clip out of her hair and as it cascaded around her shoulders it was shot through with crimson. At that moment she looked more like a movie star than a prospecting miner. I felt a sudden tension inside again and realised that, improbable as it might seem, she could mean a lot to me. And I didn't just equate it with saving my life. She hadn't noticed and carried on talking.

"Well," she said, "now that I'm lubricated, I'll tell you. At the moment I'm contracted to Balcom, but not exclusively. I do a bit of freelance prospecting between contracts; you never know what you'll find out there."

"So what do you mean? Do you live outside the cluster?" My respect for her was increasing; she was clearly a resourceful lady.

"Oh yes, my rig is self-contained and I have a small pod with an ice converter." She saw my blank look. "Think of it like a house on the back of the rig. It's basic but liveable. I can stay out for as long as I can carry food for. I've just spent two months out past the crater in the ice so I'm a bit behind the times."

That explained her lack of knowledge about Nic, but she must have had some contact as I hadn't known about the job two months ago. I decided to go with Balcom first.

"What do you know about Balcom? Do they try and kill everyone they don't like?" Her reply was non-committal: "They're a big company and you don't get to be a big company without treading on a few toes."

"Yes that's how it used to be," I agreed, "but I've heard that since Donna Markes got involved things have started to change. I know that Balcom has always had a reputation for being ruthless, but only in a business sort of way."

"You're right about that," she nodded, sipping her beer and resting the frosted bottle against the side of her head, "but recently corners have been cut. People have died or been sacked and there have been no proper investigations or comebacks. Also Tony Hays, the new boss here, is getting Balcom involved in some dubious projects, hiding profits and money laundering. And his wife is Donna Markes's sister, so he's fireproof."

She was getting more animated as she spoke, now waving the bottle about as she made her accusations. She seemed to know as much as anyone else I had talked to and her story so far was the same as the one that Al had told me earlier.

"That sounds like pretty serious stuff," I said, "but why would you care, you're only a freelancer after all?"

She didn't answer directly, just kept on ranting: "It's so wrong. Donna Markes has wormed her way into Igor Balcom's trust and taken the company over. When she made a move for Igor it was obvious that he was old and infatuated and wouldn't hear any wrong about her. He hasn't a clue about what's going on and her men are being moved into all the top jobs. He's really only a figurehead now, just to keep it respectable."

She stopped for breath; she was flushed and drank deeply from the bottle. I considered what she had said. It fitted in pretty well with what Al had told me, and the bits and pieces I had heard from the people I had met since I got here. She had got me thinking about the company itself, not just its operation on Reevis. It was true that Balcom had changed quite a bit recently: they had reorganised their operations, publicly announced the cancelling of some big projects, and put press embargoes on others. Rumours had been circulating and their reaction was seen as a way to stop the damage that their stock price was taking. It was all damage limitation.

I got a word in, before she started off again: "But how do you know all this? Are you guessing like Al and Nic and the rest of the folk I've met recently? Maybe you're all bitter because they've been sacked by Balcom since Donna Markes and Tony Hays turned up."

She gave me a look, and again didn't answer directly. "I suppose you're right to be suspicious of our motives. But I do know a few people who have been affected, and I have lost quite a bit of prospecting work because of their cost cutting, and that's the truth." She dropped her voice, "I'm sure Nic will have told you, the whole planet is rotten. He could tell you himself – where is he?"

It was time to give her the bad news.

"You don't know, do you," I said quietly and her face fell.

"What?" she asked but I think in a way she had realised.

"I'm sorry," I continued, "but Nic's dead."

The colour drained out of her face and she slumped in the couch. I went over to her and sat beside her, putting my arm around her shoulders. She leant into me and I could feel her shoulders shake as she sobbed silently. "Dead," she whispered, "how?"

So I told her what I knew, including my suspicions about the man at my door, whose name Chumna had got wrong. She was still sobbing and held me tighter.

"I don't trust that policeman Chumna," she said, "but Flanagan has always been straight up."

"I'm sorry to have to tell you. That's why we were up at the lookout today, giving Nic a proper send-off." Her face fell even further and she started sobbing again.

"He's gone completely and I never..." She pulled away. "Wait a moment, you were the one he was meeting, weren't you, you were the man who was going to put his hotel on the map. It's your fault he's dead; it's all your fault."

Before I could tell her that she had it all wrong, she had got up and started slapping and kicking at me. I grabbed her arms and held them tight. Her rage had increased her strength and she was shouting "You've killed him" over and over again and it was all I could do to protect myself. My ribs were on fire as I stopped her hitting me. She was swearing and spitting like a wild animal in her grief, tears streaming down her face.

I let her exhaust herself and her struggles eventually subsided.

She pulled away from me and stood, shaking. "This is awful news," she said, her voice brittle, "and I need to decide what to do next." Her eyes were red and tears still welled. She crossed the room and entered the bathroom, locking the door behind her. I could hear water splash for what seemed like ages, and then I thought I heard sobs but they were drowned out by the hairdryer.

Eventually she came out, a towel wrapped around her body, tucked under her arms. Her hair was dry and hung around her face like a mask.

"Are you feeling better?" It felt like such a useless comment, but I meant it.

"Thank you," she sniffed, "I needed a shower, but I couldn't find a comb." She flicked the hair off of her face and seemed to have regained control of her emotions; she must have been embarrassed by her reaction. I hoped she wouldn't blame me for the death of someone who had clearly been close to her.

She sat next to me again, the towel riding up over her thigh. I tried not to look.

"I'm sorry," she said, "I don't normally lose it in front of strangers, and I know it was unfair of me to blame you, but I've spent two months waiting to see Nic. It's what's kept me sane, knowing I can do something to get back at Donna Markes."

That seemed a strange thing to say. "What do you mean?" I asked.

"I told you I was contracted, well, I used to get a lot of work from Balcom, all over the sector, but I spoke out about some things that I thought were wrong and I was moved sideways. I was shunted out here on the promise of a job and thrown a few crumbs, but I'm stuck now. I can't get off planet and I'm watched as soon as I get in the main dome. It's not so bad out here on the farm though, so I spent most of my time off relaxing here with Nic. But every now and then you have to go into the big dome for something and I always hate it. There's a lot of exasperated ex-Balcom employees on Reevis and a lot of the placemen of Donna Markes and Tony Hays to keep us in line."

It was the same story from everyone, so either it was group paranoia or the truth.

Tash continued, "So I tend to keep out of the way most of the time. I can put up with being alone and it suits me to stay under the radar. I find enough things out there to keep me solvent. But it's about time I was honest with you. Nic didn't just want you here for the hotel review, although that was important to him; he wanted you to get information off world, in your press bag, stuff that he couldn't send any other way."

I thought of the drive I already had and wondered if she knew of its contents.

"That's all very well," I said, "but just about every group I've met on this bloody rock has a story of how every other group are the bad guys – granted most of it is anti-Balcom but they aren't the only company on Reevis, I've checked. No one has ever given me any proof of anything. Before I can write a convincing story I need solid evidence."

"Of course we both understood that," she agreed, "but just think about what Balcom has done here. They've put everyone they don't like in one place, and mixed them together with their genuine employees and placemen – with a mixture like that there's going to be some resentment and friction. And you're wrong," she continued, "all the other companies here are Balcom-owned; it just looks like they are separate."

I would have to bow to her knowledge on that one.

"I have evidence." She pulled her bag toward her and reached in, taking out a drive-store, just like the one in Nic's jacket.

"Here you are," she handed it to me, "it's all on here – the illegal payments, the fake manifests, internal memos, the lot. This is just a copy; the original is quite safe. Now can you get this somewhere it will be believed? It's taken a lot of people a long while to gather enough evidence that can't be denied. Get it to Centra and get it out in the open."

"Why can't you do it? There are plenty of chances to get off planet, or you could just post it out."

"It can't be done that way, and it's not like we haven't tried before. Like I said, I'm watched all the time as soon as I go to the main dome. Things I've tried to send before have never arrived. I can't get an exit visa either. Neither could Nic, and half a dozen others I could tell you about. The Mayor has Balcom backing; she and Tony Hays do exactly what Donna Markes says."

"So that was why Nic had wanted the hotel review," I said, "to get a journalist onto Reevis and hope he could get the story out."

"Exactly," she replied. "Like I said, I can't do it and we didn't know who else to trust. Your name came up in conversation; we thought you'd do it for us. We figured that you'd have no love for officialdom." I thought she was going to plead with me; her eyes had got wider and I thought that she would cry again.

"Look," she persisted, "Nic reckoned you were an honest journalist – his words. He said you had integrity and hadn't sold out to save yourself when things got tough." That was true, I guess; after all I hadn't jumped on the spoilt rich girl bandwagon with Layla Balcom, and I hadn't let the delegate cow me into submission.

"Thank you for the vote of confidence," I said to her, "but if Donna Markes has taken Balcom over, all this is too late."

"No," she replied furiously, "there are still some key people loyal to Igor but they are being eased out and replaced."

She passed me a small slip of paper. "Here are some names; memorise them or write them down somewhere." There were half a dozen names, and one that leapt out at me. I copied them into my diary, hiding them amongst the pages.

I gave her the list back. "What is Harris Morgan doing on that list?" I asked her. "I've very nearly been thumped by him a couple of times."

She laughed. "Harris is a pussycat. He's there because he built Reevis and he cares about what's happening to it. He pretends to hate off-worlders but it's all an act, all he really hates are Balcom stooges. He stays and pretends to be loyal to get information and pass it on to us. If he gives you any more grief, tell him Tash said he's a silly old man." I didn't feel that brave.

"Al hates him," I said.

"Well, it's a secret," she replied, her voice serious. "Please don't endanger him by letting on to Al that I've told you." I nodded; Harris was clearly more than he seemed, and not just brave in the pioneer sort of way.

"Harris will get word to the people on that list who are on Centra," she said, "tell them that you're coming and to watch out for you." She looked at me. "When are you leaving?"

"Hang on a minute, I haven't got my review done yet." I felt that I was being rushed into things, and that I had been dragged here for a different thing than I had realised, but then I thought of the story – it could restore my reputation.

"That's not important; all that matters is the drive." We had been sitting side by side as we spoke. Suddenly Tash leant into me, slipping her arm around my waist. "I don't want to be alone tonight, I can't bear it," she whispered into my ear, her breath hot on the side of my neck. "I've been alone for months and the thought of Nic lying in that bathroom is freaking me out. I can't go back to my rig and stay there."

She looked so sad and I felt annoyed that I had been the one to have to tell her. "You can stop here," I said, "I'll sleep on the couch."

She looked at me, a direct stare, the hint of a smile playing around her mouth again. "Don't be silly," she replied, "the bed's plenty big enough for two." She rose, the towel slipping off her, and then she turned off the lights.

20

I woke in the morning and she was gone. Every muscle in my body ached and my back tingled from the path of her nails. I got up and went to the drinks machine to get a coffee, and there was note propped up. In a firm hand she had written:

> *Miles, thank you for last night. I needed to be with someone but I can't be here in the morning. Now that you have the drive you're in danger and need to get away as fast as you can. Meanwhile I must go back to where I'm safe. Al or Harris can get hold of me; they know my frequency and ID.*
> *Tash x*

I sighed and drank my coffee. I felt used, like she had only spent the night with me as a reward for my agreeing to go to Centra with the drive. Maybe the tears were all an act too. But the trouble was I missed her already, and I knew that she meant more to me than she realised.

I looked at the drive, and this one was just as explosive as the one about Layla. When I opened it on my tablet there were hundreds, maybe thousands of documents. I started with the oldest and skimmed them. Taken individually they seemed mundane but there was a thread running through them and as time passed and I read more, the implication of Balcom's involvement with organised crime was impossible to hide.

I recognised the names of some of the 'businesses' that they were dealing with, all front companies for the disposal and legitimising of cash, and the transport logs confirmed shipments of 'goods' in their names. There were payoffs for contracts, and other payments for favours, all illegal.

Tony and Shelly Hays seemed to be running the scam on a day to day basis but there was input from Donna and lots of reference to 'problems', and even to the removal of key personnel.

They must have been sure of their security to commit so much to record, but given the extent of the operations I guessed they would soon lose track of what was going on without some sort of reference. Interestingly there was a list of payments to unnamed people, just a list of initials; these were probably people in customs or others who turned a blind eye.

I opened another folder on the drive and found details of the reductions in safety that Al and Tash had mentioned. However the spreadsheets showed that the budgets were kept the same – the difference must have been going somewhere.

All in all there was enough to keep a bunch of investigators in work for a few months; it was no wonder that Tony didn't want any officials looking around on Reevis.

21

So all I had to do was get off planet with the drive, but I realised that that might not be as easy as it sounded. For a start, Tash had said that the process was made more complicated by the authorities, acting on instruction from Balcom via the Mayor. But I had a secret weapon: I already had my return ticket and I had a press pass, which usually guaranteed easy movement with minimal interference. Press freedom had been hard won, but in general journalists were left alone. And as the Hays didn't want outside attention, I thought that might work in my favour.

But before I could go I had to try to get a copy of the drive off planet. I knew that I might not be so lucky this time. I was not a threat when I posted the last one, but I needed this one to go without anyone knowing it was me sending it.

I thought about it over an excellent breakfast, the outline of a plan in my mind. I remembered what Jennie the Ranger had said, how no one ever took much notice of what they were doing, and all that they wanted to do was help.

This time I was going to post two copies: one to Gaynor and one to my apartment on Centra. And I reckoned that I had worked out how to do it. Tash had said the drive was a copy but I went back to my room and made two more anyway before I set off to find the people who could help me. I got prepaid envelopes from the desk and just for a bit of extra peace of mind I asked the barman Gaz to address them for me. He looked puzzled as he did it, I didn't tell him why and he didn't ask; I wanted them to be untraceable. When he had done I set out for the main dome.

I wore the Balcom jacket and overalls, the envelopes stuffed in my pockets, and once again I managed to get a free ride through the tunnels. When I got there the place looked the same, still a good breeze blowing and still full of pigeons.

I walked around for a bit until I found a purple-jacketed Ranger; he was one that I hadn't seen before. I asked him if he could get Lance or Jennie to meet me by the museum, I needed some assistance. He gave me a suspicious look. "I'm not one of Shelly's troops," I told him. "You lot gave me these clothes a couple of days ago. Tell her it's Miles the journalist." He said that he would try but that it might take a couple of hours, would I wait in the diner?

That was fine by me. I went to the diner and got myself a coffee. Macie wasn't about and neither was Harris or Shelly, in fact the place was nearly empty. I sat in a booth facing a small group of young mothers with their children. There seemed to be a party of some sort going on.

I got out my tablet and wrote a few words. I had considered telling my side of the Layla Balcom story ever since my release; Gaynor had persuaded me that it would be popular. At first I had dismissed the idea, I didn't want to stir up any more trouble for myself, but now that I had more time to think about the idea it felt like the right time to begin. Officially I was subject to the rules about secret trials but as long as I didn't say too much about that part of it I reckoned I could get it past the lawyers. It might ruffle a few feathers.

The children were running around the diner and making a bit of a noise; it was good to hear sounds of happiness. It would have been even nicer if the whole population could be as full of innocent enjoyment. One of the women shouted, "Sorry," over to me with raised eyebrows, but I just smiled and said, "No problem."

I was on my second coffee and enjoying a pastry when someone slipped into the booth behind me. "Hi, Mr Goram," she said in that intense way I had noticed before, "Jon tells me you need something, what can we do for you?" I stopped typing and leant back, the backs of our heads nearly touching over the top of the seat backs.

"Good morning, Jennie," I said, "don't you want to sit with me?"

"No thanks," she said. "No offence – I've spotted one of Shelly's agents in the group of women over there so I don't know you."

The waitress came over and poured Jennie a coffee, they chatted briefly for a few moments, the waitress said yes a couple of times and left. "It's going to get noisy in a moment," said Jennie. "When it does tell me what you want."

Sure enough, the waitress walked over to the group and I heard her say, "Who wants ice cream?" The children gathered round and started jumping up and down, shouting, "Me, ME!" in increasing volumes, whilst the mothers called for quiet. I took my chance; I lifted my coffee cup to my lips to hide them as I spoke.

"Can you get a couple of envelopes into the post for me, so that I'm not associated with them?"

"Sure, that's easy," she replied, "give me twenty minutes then leave and walk towards the museum. Just before you get there, there's an alley between two brown buildings. The one on the left has graffiti on it. Give the envelopes to the boy coming towards you."

"And that's it?" It seemed too simple. Surely Al or anyone else could have sent the drive off world like that. "Has anyone else ever asked you to do that before?"

"No," she said and I detected anger in her voice, "most people think we're a bunch of silly kids, playing games. No one wants to believe we could do more than stop people getting beaten up. We want to make a difference; we're the future of this place."

"Well I trust you with this," I said, "and it's pretty important." But there was no answer – she had already gone.

The children were quieter now that they had their ice cream. I waited the full twenty minutes, then finished typing, rolled up my tablet and left after paying for my coffee. I walked halfway to the museum and stopped, sitting on a bench at the edge of the park. Sure enough, I soon spotted one of the women from the diner, without a child, walking towards me. I grinned to myself; if Jennie was right it wouldn't matter.

I set off again at a brisk pace, but not a guilty one, and saw the alley. The graffiti said 'Balcom Sucks!' which I thought was appropriate. I didn't look behind me, I simply turned down into the shadows.

I could see three figures coming toward me and hesitated; Jennie had only said give it to the boy. Then I saw that Jennie was in the lead, and the third figure had stopped, blocking the other end of the alley. Jennie walked past me without acknowledgement and kept going. The boy approached and I took the two envelopes from my pocket; he had an open bag in his hand and I dropped them into it.

I turned around and they were both walking towards the main road, the bag no longer visible. The third boy came past me, leant into the shadows and retrieved the bag. He walked back past me, grinning. "Wait there," he said as he passed. I looked back and as Jennie and the boy reached the road, a car pulled to a stop and several policemen appeared. They grabbed Jennie and the boy and bundled them into the car. I felt guilty and hoped that they weren't treated too roughly. The policeman looked down the alley but their view was blocked by me, so they probably couldn't see the third boy. I turned back. He had dropped the bag about ten metres in front of me and was walking out of the alley. I ignored his advice and followed him. I saw him cross the road. No one followed me or took any notice.

22

I went back to the airlock and took a runaround to the port. I found that I had to pay this time; the driver apologised and told me that Balcom hadn't settled their monthly bill so in return they were charging everyone.

When I got to the booking desk there was a queue of shouting people. I waited in line for a good half hour until it was my turn. "You're busy today," I said to the girl, who was looking harassed. "When's the next departure for Centra?" I showed her my ticket and ID.

"There's one tomorrow, Mr Goram," she said, "but I'm afraid that I can't get you a place on it; there are no cabins available for the leg from Reevis to Centra."

"But I've got a ticket," I said. Surely I hadn't been barred by someone.

"It's not just you," she waved at the irate group around and behind me, "nobody can go. There's been a convention on some world out in the sticks and everyone's coming back to Centra on this liner. It'll stop for the mail of course but there's no cabin space." At least that meant that my envelopes would be on it if the plan had worked. I tried flashing my press pass but all that got me was a shrug and another apology.

"When's the next place available?" I asked. I didn't want to be here any longer than I had to.

"The next bookable cabin I've got is in seven days," she said. "The express liner's already full with the people who can't go on tomorrow's so I'm afraid it's the slow one after that."

It would have to do. I confirmed my booking and returned

to the hotel. I didn't bother with the main dome, just went straight back through the hub to the farm.

If I had a week to waste then I could spend the time polishing my review and writing the outline of my story, even though the review was just a device to get me here and didn't need to be done. I might as well try and drum up some business for the hotel, and now was the ideal time.

Even with all my good intentions after a couple of days I was bored with writing so I decided to have a good look around the cluster, or at least the parts I could get access to.

Quite a few of the domes were restricted to Balcom employees and the runaround drivers wouldn't take me as I had no pass cards. The ones I could get to were like small industrial estates, the base for surveyors and independent contractors. There were also all the services that you would expect in the colony: plumbers, electricians and the like. Most of the people working there were happy to chat and I discovered that Tash was right and they were all either owned by Balcom or otherwise dependant on them for their business. None of them had any bad things to say about that arrangement but it was still an eye-opener to me.

A bit of careful questioning and various items in the local news showed that there were proposals for new domes, both for business and science units and for extra living space. The news sheets seemed heavily biased towards the Balcom line, that as experts in dome construction and maintenance they should have complete control. Independent comment was either lacking or was very muted, showing the control the Hays had over the settlement.

I also found by talking to Davis Muloy one evening in the hotel bar that an expansion to the farm was planned, and that a major export plan was being developed. From my visit I believed that but in general the more I saw and the more I found out, it seemed that no one told the truth in this place, only what made them appear to be the good guys.

I did bump into Lance when I was called over to the Hotel Splendid one day to talk about my bill. Despite my room being paid for up front, they had heard that I was leaving and wanted a sum of money that I considered excessive for 'damages'. I went over to tell them that I wouldn't be paying as none of it was my responsibility. We argued for a while and I threatened to call the police to back me up and eventually they relented in their efforts to shake me down, providing I paid for the contents of the fridge. Since it had been empty on my arrival I wasn't happy about that either, but when I asked them how much, it was such a small amount that it seemed to be a cheap way of solving the problem. So I paid and walked out.

When I left the building, Lance was waiting for me; he told me that my drives had made the post the same day as I handed them over. "They should be on Centra by now," he proudly announced, "we put them in different envelopes, made them look like gifts."

I asked him about Jennie and the boy. "They're OK," he said, "they were just given an interrogation but said nothing, only that they had been hanging out in the alley. Their parents had to be there as they're both under eighteen and they were warned as well. Jennie and Jon have been grounded; we don't see them anymore." He sounded sad.

"I'm sorry to put you to the trouble," I told him, "I don't want to see anyone's life ruined."

"Don't worry," he said, "their families are supportive, they all hate the way things are."

I tried to get in touch with Tash, via Al, but she must have gone back to her prospecting and was not in range. I really missed her and thought about her constantly; it was starting to worry me. I had been alone since my trial and thought I had got out of the habit of wanting to be part of a couple. Certainly

I hadn't welcomed Gaynor back with open arms and I should have. She had given me support and space which had been very understanding of her but maybe I'd needed the opposite.

Nic's hotel was really good, as good as any on the pleasure circuit. He had clearly thought about what he wanted to offer and I had no hesitation in giving it a good report.

I had got into the habit of going into the hotel bar most evenings, rather than drinking alone in my room. Every time I went into the hotel bar a beer appeared by my side, together with some peanuts. I had already seen Davis, and occasionally Al would be there and we would talk.

He had some fascinating stories about his work with the terraformers, and I managed to tell him some good yarns about my gossip columnist times, but all I really wanted to know was if he had seen or heard from Tash. Most of the time he said that he hadn't but one evening he gave me some news.

"I spoke to Tash," he said, as we sipped beer and watched the aura. "She asked if you were still here and when I said you were she sent her love." He must have seen the look of relief in my eyes; maybe her note wasn't the end.

"You got on well then," he muttered. "She also told me that she had given you the drive." He said 'the drive' as if it was the Holy Grail, a sort of reverent tone like the one that he had used at Nic's funeral.

"Yes," I agreed, "I've got it and I'm taking it to Centra in my press bag."

"Good, that's what Nic and a lot of other people want."

"Did Tash say anything else?" I tried to sound casual but I probably didn't.

Al grinned. "Lovely lady, isn't she? I could see in her eyes over the video call that you and her had hit it off. No, she didn't but she did say she was looking forward to your return."

23

One day when boredom had really set in I decided to take the tour to the cold side. It turned out to be spectacular. If there hadn't have been a hot side it would have been amazing enough, but the two together were really a wonder of the universe.

The tour was led by May, who seemed to be Al's partner in more ways than one. She had all the patter and in the lounge before we left she gave us a brief but fascinating speech about the landscape we would be seeing and the history of Reevis. A lot of it was the same as I had heard in the museum, but she said it in a much more interesting way and made it a more personal story. We didn't even have to walk from the lounge to the EV; a small runaround picked us all up.

There were a few other passengers on the tour and we chatted briefly to each other in the EV after the safety briefing whilst we waited to depart. Among them were an older couple from Alborea who had found the hotel on the hypernet. They had travelled all over since retirement, seeking out the wonders of creation – at least that's what the lady, Grace, said in the poetic speech patterns of the far worlds. Alborea was a pretty sensational place to live in its own right but they had been bowled over by the beauty of the hot side and wanted to see the contrast.

There was also a family from Centra. The parents had three children, including a daughter of around eighteen; she was moody and disparaging of just about everything, but perked up when she heard my name. "Aren't you the one who thought they had found Layla Balcom?" she asked me. Her parents looked blank.

"Yes," I carefully replied. Just then the realisation of who his daughter was talking to dawned on the father, who moved in to separate us. "Don't you ever talk to my daughter again," he hissed. "We're respectable and don't associate with criminals." I was shocked and upset by his lack of the full story and stepped back quickly. May must have heard the exchange and came back from the pilot's seat, where she had been preparing to depart.

"Do you have a problem, Mr Maris?" she sweetly asked.

"What is he," and he waved at me, "doing on here?"

"Well," she answered with a serious face, "as far as I'm aware, Mr Goram was the victim of a miscarriage of justice." I could see the daughter nodding. Mrs Maris sat stone-faced, clearly embarrassed, while the other passengers were lapping up the diversion. "If you know different, perhaps you could enlighten us." He went red and shut up, avoiding me for the rest of the day. It reminded me of the fun and games I could expect when I returned to Centra and started spreading the story.

Grace leant over and put her hand on mine. "Don't you take any notice, my lovely," she said in her kindly voice, "I know what politicians are like and what they did to you was wrong. You stick with us today." She took me under her wing and she and her husband made the trip one of the happiest days of my stay on Reevis. The rest of the passengers were mining students on a field trip; they kept to themselves and chatted on their phones for most of the time.

We left the base and headed for the Ugly Sisters. I sat back and thought of the last time I had come this way and where it had led me. It looked as spectacular as ever and after circling it we headed for the cold side.

The crater extended from the edge of the lava to the cold

side, and we ran down the line of the sunrise until we reached a solitary marker. "Ladies and gents," announced May, "we are now leaving the controlled area of the settlement; we are on our own from here." It was said for effect and there were lots of oohs and ahhs as we passed it.

We swung away from the light and pretty soon entered a field of boulders, marking the point where the glaciation had receded in some past epoch. The lights on the top of the EV showed ice, thin and flat at first but gaining in depth and pattern as we carried on. We started to climb, the wheels slipping at the loss of traction as we rose up the face of the glacier that was shown on the map display at the front of the cabin.

"If you look out of your ports on the left," said May, "you can see the route up through the ice field to our look-out post." Sure enough, a line of flashing markers rose in a series of 'S' bends to an oasis of light perched on high. "You'll be pleased to hear that I turned on the heating and the interior lights when we left our base," she continued, "it should be pleasant inside by now."

In the darkness there was no way to tell the distance, but our speed had not slowed and after a switchback ride up the slope we were in the lookout's airlock. Once again we waited for the inner door, and then we trundled into a large space. On leaving the EV, I found myself in the mirror of the lookout on the hot side, right down to the small coffin-sized lock. Everyone rushed to the dark Plastoglass wall. Stars could be seen above a dark horizon. Sure enough it was warm inside, a row of ventilators in the rock pumping out warm air.

May and her co-pilot had been connecting fuelling hoses; now she flicked a switch and the area in front of us was illuminated. There was a collective intake of breath.

The cold-side scenery was just as awe-inspiring in its own way. Instead of a sea of lava the sea was of ice, locked forever in a pattern of frenzied waves, the dirty grey colour shot through with lines of colour, bright reds and greens. These were deposits of minerals and metals, gouged from the rock by the ice during past movements of the glaciers. At least that's what May said. They showed that the planet hadn't always been like this – maybe one day it would all change again. The spectacular view was created by hundreds of high-intensity lights, all set out in a pattern that generated a stunning show. It was a good job that electrical energy was no problem; over an excellent lunch May gave figures for the power used and they were mind-boggling.

After we had finished lunch we had a drive through the ice field. A route had been carved, enlarging natural chasms, and the lights switched on and off as we passed, creating amazing effects and highlighting the formations. All the time May kept up the commentary as we cruised through the ice; we just sat in awe. In the end as we turned away and drove down the slope of the glacier it felt like we had all shared in something special. Even Mr Maris came and apologised to me on the way back.

We didn't go back the same way; instead we passed the power station, which was another wonder to behold. There was a large ceramic pipe going into it, coming from the mountains. May explained that it contained lava and was laid on a slight slope so it flowed into the plant, which had been sited here for that reason.

There was a steady stream of tugs with trailers of ice arriving at the other side; the ice was automatically unloaded into a hopper at the rear of the station. May explained that once inside the ice was crushed and passed over the lava flow. The melt was then collected up, methane was stored and the water was split into oxygen and hydrogen. All the electrical power was produced by turbines, driven by steam from a portion of the water that was directly heated. More pipes led out towards the domes. After the lava had passed through the plant, it had hardly cooled and was led into a large chasm in the surrounding rocks, where it filled the space as it cooled. Even though we couldn't get inside, the place was impressive, and May's description made us aware of its importance in keeping us all alive.

Arriving back at the hotel after the tour, I crossed the lobby towards the lift when a familiar figure detached himself from the seats and moved towards me. I hadn't seen Flanagan for a while and was more than pleased to take up his offer of a drink in the bar. Maybe I could get more out of him now that I knew more.

Gaz brought beers as soon as we arrived and nodded to Flanagan; clearly they knew each other from somewhere. The place was quiet so we sat on stools at the bar. Gaz placed peanuts within easy reach and retreated to a stool by the till.

Flanagan raised his bottle. "I understand you're off soon," he said. "Has it been fun?"

"It's been different," I told him, grabbing some peanuts before he could. "I tell you what, these are becoming an obsession."

He laughed. "You'll miss dome-made when you get on the shuttle, perhaps you should take a few packs with you."

That actually gave me an idea but I put it to the back of my mind for the moment. "Do you have any more news on Nic's killer?" I asked him.

"Nope," he put on his blank cop face, "we're getting nowhere with that. If you hadn't been in orbit I would be fingering your collar but he was dead well before you landed." But not before I should have been there as well, I thought.

"You remember I told you that I got hassled in town by three Balcom heavies?" He nodded. "Well I heard that two Rangers were arrested a couple of days ago. They were stopping the same thing happening to me again." That wasn't true but I wanted to support them.

"I know, they've been told not to take the law into their own hands again."

"Don't be too hard on them, they just wanted to help."

"I'm the law – you need anything, you come to me," he said, with the emphasis on the second part. Was he trying to give me a message?

"If I come back I may take you up on that," I replied carefully.

"Good," he nodded, pleased. "We understand each other. Now we haven't been able to notify all of the people listed on Nic's will. Do you know where I can find a Tash Perdue?"

"I've seen her," I answered, "and she knows." I could still hear her sobs and feel her warmth against me.

"OK, I'll cross her off the list."

"Where's your partner?"

"Who, Chumna? Oh, he's around. We're not joined at the hip, you know."

I got the impression that he had come to deliver a message, because after that the conversation faltered. We drank a while in silence, then he made his excuses and left.

24

Suddenly, it was time for me to leave. I had developed a love for the place, well the place outside the main dome anyway, and I would be sad to leave. In readiness I had hidden the two drives in a couple of bags of dome-made peanuts, carefully resealing them with glue. The bags now resided in one of the compartments of my press bag. Tash's list of names had been scattered in my diary and I had my review. The hotel wouldn't accept any money for my stay, despite my protests that I had been longer than I intended. "It's on Nic," was all they would say.

Al drove me across the farm to the airlock. He shook my hand. "It's been good to meet you, Miles," he said. "Just a shame that it wasn't under better circumstances."

"I know," I replied, "but I will do my best to get the story out. I may be back sooner than you expect if they won't let me leave."

"Good luck," he said, "and be careful."

I went into the airlock and pressed the call for a runaround. After a couple of minutes one popped into the dome. "Good morning," I called to the driver, who was wearing a helmet with the visor pulled down over his face, "the port please."

I threw my bags in the back and climbed in. The runaround accelerated into the tunnel and stopped in the first passing place. The light was green, which puzzled me. Then the driver took off his helmet and turned to me. My stomach lurched – it was Harris Morgan. It was time to find out just which side he was on.

"Right," he barked, "I've got you here out of the way,

and the cameras are off. We can have a little chat."

I thought of running, but I would soon get lost in the tunnels and the runaround was faster. I was really exposed. He put out his hand towards me. I cringed, expecting a blow. "Tash said to tell you you're a silly old man," I gabbled.

To my surprise he took my hand and shook it. Tash had been right.

"We'll have to be quick; I know you've got a shuttle to catch." I just looked at him.

"I owe you an apology," he said. "I'm not who you think."

"So you're not going to warn me off again?"

"Not now I know who you are. I've got this act that I keep up. I hate the way Balcom has changed and I hate Tony and Shelly Hays, almost as much as I hate Donna Markes."

"So what are you really?" I asked.

He looked embarrassed. "I don't know myself sometimes. I built this place and had more than a little influence in Balcom. When I was younger I thought I was invincible, I thought I would live forever. Then when I got older, I saw things differently. I saw that the young have the power; most of the people in charge are younger than me and think I'm some sort of relic."

His voice had dropped from the strident bark to a melancholy whisper. In the tunnel it seemed almost like the echo of a faraway conversation. I had to strain to hear him. "I know they do because that's how I thought when I was young. At first I fought against them out in the open, then it was explained to me what would happen if I didn't toe the line."

"And then what, you gave up?"

"I realised that I wasn't fireproof, that if I kept attacking them publically I'd be out, and then I'd have no influence at all. So I decided to appear to be pro the new regime, but to keep on agitating, collecting any incriminating evidence that I could and trying to protect the people that were loyal to Igor."

"But everyone thinks you're behind all the intimidation," I said, and then I remembered what Flanagan had said, 'nothing has ever been linked back to him.'

"That suits me," he said, "because it makes me appear loyal. I'm more use on the inside. I know that I'm not trusted but I'm useful as a figurehead."

"Do you know where I'm going?"

"That's why I came out here this morning, to tell you not to underestimate Donna. If you try and stir up too much muck on Centra, she has all sorts of people in her pocket. I know what happened to you before. And I don't want you to leave with ill feeling."

"Thank you," I said. "By the way, I met Shelly Hays."

"Did you now? She usually keeps well out of the light; she must be worried about you."

"She said she was your daughter."

He laughed. "If she was I would have walloped her when she was growing up. I never had kids, but if I had a daughter I'd want her to be like Tash." He paused for a moment. "She says you're OK."

I appreciated that. Up to that moment, I had wanted to think that Tash was just someone I'd met, an interesting diversion for both of us, but I suddenly realised that actually I felt more for her than that.

"Shelly is a devious bitch, she's a compulsive liar and a control freak," Harris continued. "In a lot of ways she's the same as her sister, but without the business brain that Donna has. Between them they have their claws in Balcom and some folk say that I let them."

"Not just you."

"Maybe, but sometimes I think that I've not done much to stop them and I had more sway here than most."

"Yes," I said, "and maybe if you'd tried harder then

you'd be dead or driving a dodgy skimmer or drilling holes alone on the cold side."

His eyes narrowed. "That's a sobering thought. We must get you to the port – just remember what I've said."

We drove in silence for a while.

I had come to terms with the reasoning behind me taking the drive, mostly because it should be secure in my press bag. It was true that there were so many other ways of trying to get the information off Reevis; after all, it looked like the Rangers had managed it with twenty minutes' notice, but they were all without any guarantee of success or anonymity. I wouldn't know if their plan had worked until I got to Centra.

Harris's explanation had made me realise that nobody wanted to be caught with the drive and the evidence it contained, call it self-preservation or fear of reprisal or whatever you wanted. I had seen for myself the information on it. It would probably be fatal to whoever was found with it, so it was a good job there was Miles, the jailbird gossip columnist, an expendable means of transport. And totally deniable, after all – he got it off a dead man.

We drove through the hub. "I'll take you direct," Harris said. "It'll save you messing around."

The tunnel eventually took me out into the side of the port dome. There were two shuttles sitting waiting on the hard standing. I felt relieved to see them; it meant that I was closer to getting away. "Goodbye and good luck," said Harris as I lifted my bags out. "I've a feeling that you'll be back soon, you are our best chance at the moment. Just be careful." I thanked him for his honesty and walked towards the departure lounge.

I presented myself at the check-in desk but before I could put my bags in, two customs agents stopped me and escorted me to a side room. There they proceeded to take my luggage apart, and then they made me strip and examined my clothing. Next they brought in a mobile scanner, which they ran over my naked body.

They found the two brand-new drive-stores I still had and confiscated them with a shout of triumph. That didn't bother me as they were blank anyway. I hoped that their discovery would make them think they had succeeded in stopping me taking any information off planet and distract them from the contents of my press bag.

Theoretically my press bag was excluded from any customs search by treaty, as long as I signed a disclaimer to say that the contents were for journalistic purposes only, but they ignored this protocol and my protests and opened it anyway. I had disguised Tash's list in my notebook, and the original drive-stores from Nic and Tash were in the bags of nuts, together with my diary, scraps of paper, cuttings, fluff and rough notes. My continual protests were enough to stop them from looking too closely. They picked up the peanuts and inspected the bags, but replaced them without comment.

Despite their telling me I would be held, I somehow thought that they were acting above their authority and that if anyone was watching they would notice my shouting.

I was right, as the door opened and an officer came in. To my surprise he was followed by the Mayor, who looked coolly around the piles of my gear strewn over the floor and then at my nakedness. To her credit she blushed.

"This is an outrage," I shouted at her. "I'm an accredited journalist and have a press bag that your goons have opened. I've signed the convention waiver, which has been ignored. And I want my gear repacking. Do you understand what that means?"

She looked at the guards and they shrugged. "We found two drive-stores; other than that, we have no reason to hold him," the senior one said.

To my surprise, she agreed. "I'm sorry," she said, "I officially apologise that your press bag was opened." That meant that the whole thing had been recorded; the apology was a covering manoeuvre. "We have a security situation in progress," she continued, passing me my trousers, "and of course we will put your things back in the case. Do it," she ordered the guards and they sullenly complied.

"However, Mr Goram," she continued, holding up the drives, "it would appear that we may have stopped you taking proprietary information off planet. We will examine these and, if our suspicions are correct, you will be arrested on a charge of industrial espionage. We could hold you here while we do that but personally I would be more than happy to see you leave. If necessary they can sort you out when you arrive on Centra. Whatever we find, it would be wise of you if you did not return."

"Are those your words or Balcom's?" I asked and her tone changed.

"You asked me a question like that once before. Don't push your luck. Goodbye," and she turned and left.

My gear was repacked and after I had dressed I was escorted to the departure lounge and checked in. The lounge was full of people and I had to stand.

25

The shuttle for the outer worlds was called and the crowd thinned. Pretty soon there was only myself and one other person left in the lounge, a thin blond man working on a shielded tablet. The blank side of the holoscreen had the Balcom crest on it and he was typing furiously.

He glanced up and seeing that I was the only other person waiting, waved his hand, before returning to his task. The last person I wanted to talk to was another Balcom stooge so I ignored him and settled down with a beer that I had liberated from my room and the customs had left in their search.

I was enjoying the beer when I saw the man get up, pack his tablet away and walk towards me. He reminded me of a bird, walking quickly, his eyes flicking from side to side, alertly checking out the surroundings.

"Hi," he said, "I'm Tony Hays." He didn't give me a chance to say anything but kept talking, which was a good job really as I was lost for words. I could smell that aftershave again, the one I had last noticed in the Mayor's office. I knew I had smelt it somewhere before and then it came back to me: the policeman outside my hotel room whose name Chumna had got wrong.

"I'm a junior dome engineer, and I'm off to Centra to see head office," he told me. "I've been called back at short notice – juniors get all the run-around, don't they? It's a real pain in the proverbial. No one else wants to go but they never consider that you might be in the middle of something."

I muttered sympathetic words and smiled politely. Just then our shuttle was called for boarding. He was still talking, "It looks like we're the only passengers this time around." Sure enough, no one else had arrived; in fact, apart from the staff in the lounge there was only a handful of people, most of which must be waiting to meet the arriving passengers as none of them were taking any notice of the departure announcement. I didn't fancy sharing the flight with him, knowing what I did, but to ignore him would be the height of rudeness and give the game away. I would just have to be careful.

We moved through the gate where our passes were checked again and into the walkway, an airtight tube linked to the shuttle. I had my last look at the grey rocks of Reevis with the red glow behind the cliffs as I walked onto the ship for the ride into orbit.

As we boarded the stewardess made a fuss of Tony Hays and ignored me; hopefully he would get a good seat and I could be anonymous down the back. But we were seated together across the aisle in the middle of an empty craft.

After settling into the seats and strapping in we endured the safety briefing, and I thought of Al and the briefing I had never had in his EV. As usual it did little to reassure me; all it really said was, 'We have to carry escape pods, but it's unlikely that you'll get to them before your blood boils away in the vacuum.'

As we climbed away from the cluster, I could see the scale of the settlement compared to the surroundings. It looked so insignificant, as if it couldn't have any influence on anything.

We banked away from the hot side; a view of the lava sea filled my port and as we rose further the ribbon itself made a striking division between the red side and the dirty white side. The cluster was still visible as a small dot, nestled in the lee of the cliffs surrounding the crater.

As the planet dropped below us, I began to feel relief that I had got away with all my stuff intact, but apprehensive about what would be waiting for me on Centra.

I must have let out a sigh of relief, as Tony leant across his seat towards me. "You sound pleased to be leaving." He was trying to start a conversation but I didn't really feel like talking to him. However I reckoned I'd better try and chat; he didn't know that I knew who he was.

"It wasn't what I was expecting when I arrived," I agreed, "but in a strange way I'm sad to be going."

"What was her name, Miles?" he said and must have noticed my shocked face. "Oh," he said at my reaction, "I was only joking, and not meaning to pry."

"That's alright." I tried to keep my emotions in check. Tash was down there in danger because of this man and I desperately wanted to get things finished so that I could get back to her. "Sorry to disappoint you," I answered, "there was no woman. I wish there had been, just a few things happened that I didn't expect."

"Ah yes, well you caused a few ripples; it must be an occupational hazard for someone in your line of work."

I suddenly realised that he had used my name though I had never mentioned it. Not only that, he had just shown that he knew more about me than he could have found from the passenger list. Of course he knew who I was; maybe he thought that I was unaware of his importance. He must be sending me the message that he knew all about me, that I was in his sights.

"Excuse me," I told him, "I don't mean to be rude but I'm a little tired. I wonder if I can move over to one of the recliners." I pointed to a row of seats behind me.

"I don't think so," replied Tony. "We're seated to even the weight out; I believe it's quite important on shuttles."

I didn't like him; he was too smooth and sure of himself.

I wouldn't have liked him even if I hadn't known about him and didn't trust myself not to show it, so I merely smiled, nodded and tipping my seat back pretended to sleep.

The liner was on time, appearing ahead of us like a gigantic black sheet, covering the stars. As we approached a huge door slid open in its side and we flew into the docking bay. Liners never entered atmosphere, they were just too big to be subjected to the stress of re-entry. Without that constraint they could be any size once the trans-light engines and field generators had been fitted; the bigger they were, the more passengers and freight they could carry, maximising profits. They were Balcom designed and built, by another arm of the company that I had found out so much about in the last few days. They circled the inhabited worlds, never stopping, like sharks always on the move with nowhere to call home.

I had never really given it much thought before, but now I could begin to see the power the company had over everyday life.

When the bay had pressurised we left the shuttle and walked into the passenger spaces. The baggage was being unloaded by the liner's crew, along with the mail and stores. It would be filled with departing passengers and return mail, leaving again before we set off for Centra.

Tony and I entered the passenger space where cabins were assigned; he was in the premier class and on a different deck to me. That was a relief; it made it less likely that I would see him on the trip. "See you again," he cheerfully said as he was taken to his cabin. My more modest berth was down in the economy class, full of miners and tourists.

After the shuttle had departed, we left the orbit of Reevis and accelerated to light speed once we were clear of the planet's gravity. Some people claimed to never notice the transition to light speed but I always got the feeling of a kick in my stomach that told me we were disproving the greatest minds on old Terra.

Even though the premier-class passengers had their own facilities, I decided that it would be wise to keep out of Tony Hay's way, so I seldom left my cabin, which was fine as there was everything there that I needed. I ate in the cheap restaurant, avoided the bar and only spotted him a couple of times on the trip.

I used the time to complete my report on the travel arrangements for any prospective tourist to Reevis. I was glowing about the hotel and the facilities, gave Al a good plug for his tours, but summarised by saying that the overall atmosphere was that of an industrious and insular society, where strangers were not immediately welcomed. I thought that was a fair assessment. Then I got on with my book. It was hard going, as it brought a lot of things back to me, and I compensated with the contents of the cabin fridge. But it kept me out of the way.

After five days and a couple of stops we arrived in orbit above Centra, the capital planet of the Federation and my home. Looking down at its blue and green surface, dotted with clouds on the day side and patches of light and dark on the night, I almost missed the lack of a dome. All my life was down there, all the good and the bad. Part of me wanted things to go back to the way they were but part of me wanted life to carry on, to prove that I could rise above all the adversity.

Again we went through the process of joining a shuttle, a much more crowded one this time, for the trip down to the surface. I hadn't spotted Tony Hays so maybe he had already left; there had been a shuttle before the one I was assigned to.

After all the passengers had been transferred, and new ones, along with stores and maybe a crew change, the liner would carry on in its perpetual circuit of the inhabited worlds.

As we dropped down through the clouds, in the buffeting of re-entry, I was surprised to find that I wasn't feeling quite as worried as usual. I didn't have the feeling that the shuttle would explode around me; my anxiety seemed to have been calmed by my recent experiences. I actually enjoyed the sensation.

There were long queues for customs, but here my press pass was respected and I only suffered a cursory examination. I told the officer that I had come from Reevis and he shuddered – clearly he didn't fancy living under a dome. No arrest warrant could have been sent from Reevis as immigration waved me through and I was soon free to leave the spaceport.

Once in the open air I walked towards the queue for the taxis. It felt strange to see the suns high in the sky and feel real wind on my face. Now that I had got here, and all the information I carried was intact, I couldn't decide what to do next. I realised that I didn't have a plan. Obviously I couldn't just rush off and show the drive to Igor Balcom – I needed some help. Should I see Gaynor first or try and find one of Tash's contacts? In the end I decided to see Gaynor.

As we drove into the city, I revelled in the lack of a dome and in the blue sky overhead. It was early summer and the trees were just getting into leaf, the air was warm and you didn't have to rely on technology for your next breath. Even when it rained at least it would be random and not programmed. After the dome, the sheer number of people and vehicles made me almost long for the quiet beauty of the lookout.

26

We pulled up outside the offices of Gaynor's publishers. I realised that I didn't know if she was even in the building but I had to start somewhere. I hadn't called ahead because I wanted to surprise her. I paid off the cab with my card and went in. I went through security, who told me that she was in her office, so I rode the lift up to the forty-fifth floor and walked down the familiar corridor, lined with framed prints of the covers of *Getaway*. No physical copies of the magazine existed but, as she said, 'You can't hang a holoscreen on the wall every time you produce a masterpiece.' I passed her secretary, who smiled, and went into her office without knocking.

"Hi, Miles!" she screamed when she saw me. About my height, slim with purple hair and an elemental energy, she ran round the desk and grabbed me, holding me tight. "How's my favourite freelancer?"

Her office looked over the business district and looking over her shoulder as we embraced I could just make out the Balcom building as it towered over everyone else. It had been designed to make a statement and it did: *Look at me*, it screamed, *I'm bigger than all of you!*

"Good to be back," I told her as we separated.

"Sit down, I'll get us coffee. Tell me all about it." The same old Gaynor, never stopping. "Sandy," she called out, "bring us some coffee please. Go on then, spill."

I took a deep breath. "Well Nic is dead, and the planet is split into groups, all of them hate each other and they all wanted me to tell their side of the story. It's hard to know who to believe but I think I've got a real scoop for you."

She grinned. "I heard about Nic, and that upset me. I'd met him several times while he was getting finance and I know just how much the hotel meant to him. Oh by the way, I got your two envelopes. I kept the first unopened, although it killed me not to have a peek. Then when the second one turned up I couldn't understand it cos it's not my birthday. I thought you'd gone a little crazy under that dome, till I opened it up – where did you get all that information?"

It was my turn to grin. "Pretty explosive stuff eh! I thought that they would be safer coming separately, and after my press bag was opened by customs I was right."

She looked shocked. "That's outrageous! Did you complain?"

"Till I was blue, and as I was naked after a full body search it was quite difficult to keep a straight face. Then the Mayor turned up and it all got sort of smoothed over. There were some trumped up charges and I was advised not to return." Her eyes had got bigger and she shook her head in disbelief.

"We need to speak to the council about the violation of the treaty," she said seriously. "We fought for press freedom and I don't want to let it slip away."

I didn't want a long investigation to deflect me from the reason that I was here. "We can do that later, it's important that I get this story out."

The coffee arrived and she told me that she had already copied the drive onto her mainframe; now it would be archived in the magazine cloud and almost impossible to delete. I took the drive-store and the envelope and put them in my pocket.

"I guessed you would have had a look – please keep it to yourself till I'm ready to go into print."

She assured me that she would. "But don't leave it too long, its dynamite, Miles," she said, with the hunger of a real crusading journalist. "The Balcom stuff could destroy the company."

I thought that I'd change the subject. "What do you remember about Layla Balcom?" I asked.

Instantly her mood changed. "Of course I remember her but I would have thought that you would want to steer clear?"

"Hey don't blame me, I just walked into it. Anyway Nic believed she was on Reevis and he had some proof. That was on the first drive I sent, the one you haven't opened."

I explained the story about Nic's body in the bathroom and my eventful time at the Hotel Splendid. "It's all a bit circumstantial but of course I couldn't ask him about it." She nodded. "And then all the other Balcom stuff happened and it turns out that it was the real reason Nic wanted me on Reevis. Finding Layla was incidental. The person I got the Balcom stuff from wants me to present it to Igor; to show him that his beloved Donna is destroying his company."

"I'm not surprised," she said, "Donna has always had a reputation, putting it mildly. No one knows where she came from, but suddenly she was in control and it puzzled a lot of people. She seemed to wrap Igor round her finger. The government would never let Balcom fall though; they control planets, and all the technology, and that's the problem."

"How do you mean?" I asked.

"It's all right exposing wrongdoing but have you considered what would happen if Balcom failed? Is it really in anyone's interest to ruin all that?"

I hadn't thought of it in that way. I had assumed that all that would happen was that Donna Markes would be arrested and Balcom would go back to how it was, with Igor running things honestly. But considering what I had learned, if all the honest managers had been replaced who would run it? I thought of Tash's list; there were hardly enough names on it to fill a shuttle, never mind anything else.

"Igor can run things, and there must be a few—"

She interrupted me: "Igor's sick and while you've been on Reevis the stock price has wobbled." That was news to me and changed things, made them more urgent.

"I didn't know that." I hadn't taken into account that Igor was no spring chicken.

"They have powerful friends in the business community, and in the press," Gaynor continued. "All this had better be right, or you will be looking at the wrong end of the law again." I realised that and it brought back all the memories, but Gaynor hadn't been on Reevis and seen it for herself. I was more sure this time than I had been over the Dalyster fiasco.

"But it all points to Donna and the Hays working without Igor's knowledge," I said. "All the documents support that. If Igor could disassociate himself, he might just be able to use his reputation to ride the storm. Big favour time – can you help me in getting to see him?"

"I can try," she answered, "although he's rarely seen in public, and he might not want to after last time. Leave it with me. Where are you staying?"

I would have to go back to the apartment. "At my place."

"You could always stop with me." She raised an eyebrow. "Your stuff is still there."

I was tempted – we had been a casual item – and then I thought of Tash, crying in my hotel room. In fact I was think-ing of Tash more and more as time went on. But I didn't want to spoil things with Gaynor after all she had done for me.

"Thanks," I said, "but I gotta check the place over, it's been a while."

"Be safe, Miles," she said as I left. "I'll call you when I've set up the meeting."

I left the building; clouds had covered the sky and it had started to rain.

I took a remote cab to my apartment building, revelling in the proximity of other traffic, and the incisive driving of the automatic taxi. The roads were programmed into the AI and satellite tracking computed the route. It was a brief blur of travel to my stop. I waved my card at the payment reader and the door opened. Dragging my bags I walked through the rain into my building lobby.

The place was just as I had left it, untidy and with an unloved air about it. It was all I had left; after my conviction the yacht and all my possessions had been sequestered, or sold to pay the bills. The apartment was my parent's property and had therefore been exempt from seizure.

I rarely stayed here more than a couple of nights and it always felt like too much effort to cook for one, so I tended to eat out or order in. I had hardly used the cooker since I'd taken the place over from my mother, when old age and a fading memory made her single occupancy a hazard.

I couldn't find any food that wasn't rotten, but I had my dome-made peanuts so I ate them and thought of being back on the farm or in the lookout, before dropping off to sleep as I sifted through the mail. I was glad to see that the other drive had arrived. I could see what Lance and Gaynor had meant: it screamed 'Happy Birthday' at me and was so conspicuous that no one would give it a second thought.

Next morning I awoke with a stiff neck and looking out of the window saw that it was a clear morning. The suns shone through a thin layer of cloud and after a look on my computer screen I saw that it would be perfect sailing weather. My thoughts turned to lazy days by the water, or sailing with my friends, until with a jolt I remembered that that had been before; now apart from Gaynor I was on my own. I was grateful that she had stuck with me through all the grief, and I felt guilty that I had turned her down yesterday. Truth was, although I hardly knew Tash, she had started something in me; the thought that she had sent her love via Al meant that it felt wrong somehow to rekindle my relationship with Gaynor.

I had to kick my heels until she arranged my meeting and spent the first part of the day getting the boring things done. I put a load of laundry in the washer, threw away all the rotting food from the fridge and cupboards and walked to the local shop for some milk and bread.

Back in my front room, looking out over the city from the balcony, I idly typed Tash Perdue into my computer. I hadn't even thought of doing it before, but I suddenly wanted to know everything about her. I realised that I knew nothing about her except her name, which was not a lot to go on. I would probably need the power of the magazine library, which I had to log into via my desktop machine to sift the search. There were about three million hits for the name, mainly escorts and clubs to be honest, but by adding the words 'Reevis' and 'prospector' I narrowed it down to one.

Tash Perdue was twenty-six and came from the wilds of Dandri, a large rocky planet way out in the spiral arm. She had shown an interest in geology at an early age and won a scholarship to the School of Mining and Surveying on Terra. That was the oldest and most prestigious college in the sector, the one that predated space flight and was the Alma Mater of the greats. She had graduated in the top five percent of her year and had set off to gain experience. There was no photograph, which was a little strange, but an impressive list of jobs. Being an assistant to both Laithwaite and Charles showed that her work was respected. Then it said that she had been headhunted by Balcom. She was listed as currently self-employed on Reevis.

The day passed slowly and I was tempted to call Gaynor. I didn't think I'd have long to wait, I knew what Gaynor didn't. I knew that I wouldn't have any trouble getting my meeting; after all, Tony Hays knew I was coming and Donna must have been told. They both would have an inkling that I had the drive and were probably wondering what I was up to.

Mid-afternoon, I was snoozing when the phone rang.

"Hi. It's Gaynor," she trilled. "I've set up a meeting with Donna Markes, that's the best I can manage. Be at the Balcom building at nine in the morning. Good luck."

That would have to do. I might be able to persuade her to let me see Igor but if everything else was true, it was Donna who would want to see me. And probably make sure that I didn't leave again. With that cheerful thought in mind I made a few notes about how I could approach the subject and slept on it.

27

Next morning I put on a clean suit and presented myself at Balcom's offices. The Balcom building was the tallest one in the city, at over one hundred and fifty stories. It had been specially designed to deflect the winds around its top levels with fins and arches that glittered in shining metal. The lobby was vast and marble floored, with display cases containing things from their diverse interests: the first ever hyper-drive tube, a rock from some planet I had never heard of, a bust of Igor's grandfather, that sort of thing.

My press bag wasn't searched but I opened it anyway, for the CCTV camera's benefit. Inside was only my notebook. Both drives were in my pocket. I was waved through the scanner and given an ID badge. It occurred to me then that I should have tried to contact at least one of the names on Tash's list. In my haste I had gone rushing off into the lion's den with no backup – only Gaynor knew where I was.

A tall imposing woman dressed in a charcoal-grey suit came towards me. "Good morning, Mr Goram. I am Donna Markes, Mr Balcom's PA. Igor has mentioned your name in the past." She had an expression of distaste, the corners of her mouth turned down, as if I was an unpleasant article that required removal. "How can I help you?" She looked much older than she had in the video just a year ago. Her dark hair was scraped back from a strong forehead and she wore the air of a competent high-level executive. I could see a resemblance to Shelly, the same hair and eyes and sense of entitlement. But these eyes were hard and cold.

"Good morning to you," I replied. "I'm sure Gaynor Rice

explained; I'd like to see Mr Balcom."

Her face was impassive. "I'm afraid that won't be possible, Mr Goram. Mr Balcom is currently unwell and not giving interviews. Perhaps you can give me some idea what it's about and I'll try to help you."

I almost said, 'Yes, it's about your criminal empire and your embezzling brother-in-law', but instead I said, "No, it's personal for Mr Balcom. I'm sorry to hear of his illness and of course I understand his reluctance to see me. I can always tell my editor that you would not let me see him. The magazine will be publishing the story I have anyway but I thought that it would be courteous to tell him what I will be saying before I say it."

She looked amused. "That's an interesting scenario, Mr Goram, but you see Balcom doesn't really care what gossip you print; indeed, our lawyers could probably stop it and ruin you if we wanted. Your editor, Gaynor somebody, well she would find it very hard to get another job after we had finished." She looked at me. "I'm sure you will know how that feels."

She stopped for a moment. "I understand you were just on Reevis."

"That's right, and yes it's true that I have met Mr Balcom before. As well as some personal news for him I've brought back some amazing stories from Reevis that I think would fascinate him – perhaps you would like to hear them?"

I saw a flicker in her eyes. "As I thought," she said, "more half-truths and gossip – nothing to concern a company of Balcom's size."

I nodded. "Hopefully that's very true, and if the information I had was what you say then that would be possible. But I have more than enough to blow your empire apart, more than you could ever hope to cover up. It's getting published, whether you like it or not!"

I wondered if I had made more of a target of myself but after a long, hard gaze she shrugged. "Very well, see Igor if you must, but you might not get much sense from him." Her voice was triumphant. "After you've seen him you'll realise that I'm in charge now."

She took me to a private lift, away from the main lobby. "This will take you direct to the penthouse," she explained as she used a card to call the lift. "You'll have to excuse me, I have some things to arrange. Call the lift when you're done, and if the nurse tells you to leave, that's it." I wasn't expecting her to leave me alone with Igor; he must be really sick. And the things to arrange sounded ominous, but I was stuck with it and she knew that.

"Goodbye, Mr Goram," she said as the lift doors closed. We shot up to the top floor with a speed that took my breath away. There were no controls on the lift, just a keyhole under the floor display. We arrived and a door opened onto a small lobby. There was a single window looking out over the city and a door. A plant grew in an old blue and white vase from Terra.

I knocked but when there was no answer I tried the door; it was unlocked and I went into the penthouse.

The rooms were enormous and looked out far above all the other buildings; I could see the blue line of the ocean in the distance. They were full of furniture and more priceless ornaments, but everything was covered with plastic sheeting, as if the apartment was closed for the winter. I saw things that I remembered from my last visit over two years ago, and they looked like they hadn't been moved. I walked through the rooms till I got to the master bedroom. I pushed the door open.

Igor Balcom, master of the largest concern in the sector, lay propped up in bed, his breath rasping. He looked shrunken but his eyes were bright. There was a nurse fiddling with something at the side of the bed and she looked up as

I stood in the doorway. "Stop right there. Who are you?" she asked, her eyes moving to a buzzer by the bed. "What do you want here?"

When I didn't immediately answer she moved to stand; arms folded, between me and the bed, like an animal defending her young. She was tiny but radiated authority.

"Donna?" called a voice from the bed.

"It's alright," I answered, holding my hands out, showing her the inside of my bag, "Donna sent me up to see Mr Balcom."

"Donna," the voice repeated, sounding frightened.

"Give me your bag," she demanded; she took it and looked inside. Then she dropped it and stood to one side.

"Very well but not too long, he is very weak and a bit confused today," she said. She turned to the bed and placed the buzzer by Igor's side, whispering a few words. Then she walked towards me. "I will be outside listening. If I hear any shouting, or he buzzes me I will be back with security and then you'll have to leave."

"Thank you," I said and she nodded briefly.

"Who are you? Where's Donna?" Igor called out again as I approached the bed, his voice shrill and wavering. A few strands of his once thick brown hair lay limp across his head.

"Mr Balcom, I am Miles Goram." His face showed that he recognised the name.

"You," he said, "what do you want now, have you come to tell me more lies?"

"I think you are mistaking me, sir; I was always fair in respect of your daughter."

He snorted, "And now she's gone, Donna has reminded me." This was not going well.

I tried to start again: "I have found some things out about your company, sir, bad things, and I wonder if you are aware."

"You need to speak to Donna, she handles Balcom now," was his reply. The voice was stronger, more like I remembered it.

"It's about the way she runs Balcom," I said.

"Are you threatening me?" He coughed, and reached for the mask by his side. Taking a few deep breaths seemed to strengthen him. "Well, are you?" he asked again.

"No, sir, I would not do that, but your loyal employees are concerned about the influence Donna has over you." For a moment he looked sad, then he coughed again and his body shook.

"How dare they? Donna and I are in love, and will formalise our relationship when I recover." He coughed again, and it sounded to me like the cough of a dying man. "Donna runs the company now, and she should be here to hear these accusations." He scrabbled weakly at the buzzer, his hand spotted with age, the tendons and veins standing out on the thin limb.

"Wait," I said, "I also have news about Layla."

"Hah," he laughed, "you said before that you'd found her, with the delegate, but it was all lies, and you were punished for your lies, yes, punished." He stopped and struggled for breath, wheezing, "Now you come back with the same story. Why should I believe you this time?"

I was just about to tell him when the nurse came in. "You called me, Mr Balcom?" she asked in a concerned tone. Seeing his distress she ordered me out, threatening to call the building's security guards. I didn't want to wait for them so I left with my dignity intact and I got back into the lift. It seemed like Donna was in charge – it felt like Igor would never run Balcom Industrial again.

28

I stood in the lift as it started to descend and considered my options. Igor had been dismissive and although that may have been confusion, he was obviously unwell. Donna seemed triumphant; after all, I was in her lair, and I just hoped that I would get out again. Then I realised that in my haste to leave I had left my bag in the room. I patted my pockets; I still had the two drives.

To my surprise, the lift stopped halfway down and I was joined by two dark-suited men; they had the air of security guards. As the lift doors shut, one of them inserted a key into the control panel.

"What's going on?" I asked.

"Don't you worry, Mr Goram, we're just taking you to see someone."

Once again I had rushed off to see Igor Balcom without covering my back. This time it wasn't the police that had got me.

The floor display went through zero, and stopped at minus two. This must have been what Donna meant when she said she had 'things to arrange'; it was beginning to look like I wasn't getting out so easily after all.

The lift doors opened onto a car park. The lighting was dim and flickering across rows of vehicles in bays, the air smelt of grease and damp. The cars were all marked on the side with the Balcom logo; there were rows of driverless vehicles like the taxi I had used yesterday and some country cars, ones that could be driven manually in or out of the city.

The two men stood one on each side of me, and grabbed an arm each. "We're going down there," they said, indicating a gap between the rows, "there's a man wants to see you."

My feet were lifted off the ground and I was carried towards a man sitting on a car. As we approached him I recognised his face in the flickering light: it was the man from the liner, Balcom's manager on Reevis, Tony Hays. He still wore the same smug expression and juggled a leather-bound cosh in his hands.

"Hello, Mr Goram," he said, "we meet again. I've been watching you and we seem to have a problem – you are asking too many questions and now you've been frightening an old man. So what do you really know?" He waved the cosh and I was released, my feet touched the ground. I shook my arms around to get the feeling back.

"Me, I'm just writing a hotel review. I thought you said you were just an engineer."

"Ah, but neither of us are being totally honest are we?" He had a bored, flat voice, speaking as if he was lecturing a small child. "My friends on Reevis tell me that you're poking about in old news, making waves. Remember what happened to you before – this time it could be worse."

So he knew who I was, and my history. I said nothing. He seemed to want to talk; perhaps he enjoyed dragging my discomfort out. If it delayed the pain a bit, I was all for it.

"My friends here are itching to explain things a little better," he said, "but they are well trained and will wait for my instructions." Beside me the two grunted.

"Who are you then?" I asked. "Are you Mr Tony Hays, Balcom's man on Reevis or are you Officer Levson, policeman and guard?"

"I'm impressed," he said, "how did you know it was me? I kept my face away from you. I had to stand in that bloody corridor most of the bloody night, all because my bloody wife couldn't organise the theft of a bloody drive-store from a man without killing him."

"The aftershave," I explained, "it's very distinctive."

"It should be," he said, "it's expensive enough. Shelly is always reminding me how much it costs."

"I smelt it in the Mayor's office as well," I said, and he looked even smugger.

"Yes, she's a fine woman isn't she, a nice diversion – but don't let on, it might not go down too well." He winked conspiratorially.

"That's more dishonesty from you. I can't say I'm surprised, but don't you mean Harris Morgan's daughter?" This amused him, and he chuckled.

"That's her sense of humour, stupid old fool that he is." His dismissal of Harris really annoyed me.

"And just how many planets have you colonised, Tony?" I said sarcastically.

This must have touched a nerve because the smug façade dropped and he coloured. He started shouting, his voice echoing around the space, "I'm as good a man as him and better than you. Harris Morgan is cannon fodder, he's like a carthorse, strong in the muscle but no appreciation of politics. That's what made him easy to control. I know he hates me and I've managed to get him to hate to order. He knows he's only alive because of me and that keeps him loyal." He paused for breath, his shoulders shaking and his face flushed.

I thought of Harris Morgan's anguish in the tunnel, how he had wrestled with his conscience before doing what he did, and his record of bravery for Balcom. He was a better man than Tony Hays, and Tony Hays knew it.

"Have you ever considered that respect is a better way of dealing with people?" I said calmly. He laughed at that; the anger had faded again, replaced by the smug complacency.

"It's never as effective as fear. Let's get down to business.

Search him." One man moved behind me and grabbed both my arms. The other rummaged in my pockets. He pulled out the two drives and handed them over to Tony.

"Two," he said. "I know about one, what's on the other? Never mind, we'll find out soon enough."

"I suppose that now you've got the drives back you're going to warn me off." I tried to hope but knew that was unlikely.

"Oh no, Mr Goram, I'm going to kill you," he continued in the same bored voice. "It's a bit unfortunate you getting out of the lift on the wrong floor and then disturbing some thieves in our car park." He indicated the two. "These two thieves here to be precise. And it will all be filmed on CCTV. Of course they're wearing masks so I doubt that they will get caught. Especially as we can always edit the footage."

As he spoke the two pulled ski masks from their pockets and put them on. The flickering lights added to the feeling of impending doom. It was like a bad movie, and Tony's lack of emotion made it all the more frightening.

My bowels suddenly felt full of liquid. I started to sweat, even though it was cold in the car park. "You'll never get away with it; Gaynor Rice knows I'm here." That remark had no effect on his demeanour; he acted as if it didn't matter.

"I'm sure she does but don't you worry, Donna Markes will tell all about it and even show her the footage. You can relax in the knowledge that we aren't going to kill her, your last thoughts won't be that her death is your fault. Meanwhile I will be going back to Reevis to tidy up the loose ends, and then my life will return to normal."

I thought of Tash being a loose end but kept quiet about her.

"What do you mean, loose ends?" I was trying to keep living for a little while longer.

"Since you ask, we know you haven't got any physical

evidence other than the drive and I've got that now. Our tame supporters will make sure your allegations are soon forgotten. Do you think Donna is stupid? She's had a plan from the start. She's put all her enemies in one place, all the troublemakers and Igor loyalists, now we only need a little accident and all her problems will have disappeared."

His eyes had glazed over with some kind of manic zeal; the power had clearly gone to his head. His rant continued, "The insurance will finance a new dome and she's blameless. She can cry a little and have a big memorial – a bit of money to the families and they will be so grateful for her munificence they won't question it. Then no one will be able to stop her. Hold him," he said, swinging the cosh, "I'll just warm him up a bit for you."

I was stunned by that. The thought of all the people in the dome dying so that a criminal operation could continue was staggering. I thought it was a good idea not to mention that Gaynor had a copy of the drive – if they were prepared to destroy the domes at Reevis, then Gaynor was expendable; at least this way she would escape with her life. The two grabbed me again and pulled my arms out, kicking my feet apart so that I stood spread-eagled.

I knew then that I was going to die. I felt nothing but sadness, for Tash, Gaynor and everyone on Reevis. I could hear a faint sound, like a car coming into the car park; perhaps I could attract their attention and get away. As a last act, and to gain a little time, I wanted to wipe the smug smile off of Tony Hays's face, even if it was with a lie. As Tony moved towards me, I made my play.

29

"What I don't understand is why would you want to kill Nic over a story about Layla Balcom?"

"What are you on about?" he said, sounding truly mystified. He stood still, the cosh swinging. "Why would I want to know about the Balcom bitch? She's long gone. The drive that Nic had was the one about Balcom and illegal payments, and now I've got it. And once I see what's on it, I can decide how to discredit it."

"Tony, you're a fool," I said. "You killed Nic for the wrong drive; I only found the other one when I started investigating, and I wouldn't have done that if Nic had been alive." I knew that didn't fit but wanted to shake his confidence.

He just looked at me, open-mouthed; the cosh had stopped swinging and he just stood in front of me. I carried on, "If you hadn't killed Nic, I would have got the drive about Layla Balcom and done my hotel review. I probably would have left Reevis none the wiser about your empire of crime. You really screwed up."

"You're lying," he said, but he didn't sound convinced. As I was about to rub it in, the engine noise suddenly increased and a large car drove in, screeching to a halt beside me. The windows were tinted and I couldn't see inside. The two men holding me reached for the weapons they must have had in their pockets.

I saw a flicker of movement off to one side of me and as I tried to turn there was a sound like a muffled cough. At the same time as the cough I heard a noise like I imagined the cosh would soon be making on my body. I felt both of the men shudder and go limp; they let go of me and fell, leaving Tony Hays looking bewildered. Water dripped in the silence.

The car's front window opened. "Get in, Miles," said the driver, "if you want to get out of here alive." Tony was grabbed by a large man, probably the same one who had shot the two holding me, and was bundled into the back of the car.

I didn't really think about it, I could have been getting into a worse situation, but whoever it was knew my name so I ran round and jumped in the front passenger door. As I slammed it we accelerated away, sliding around the corners and up towards the daylight.

"It's your lucky day," said the driver as we bounced out of the car park, our floor scraping on the metal of the exit ramp, sending up a stream of sparks. "Harris asked me to keep an eye out for you and help if I could. I found out that you were coming to see Donna and thought you would end up down here with those two. A lot of people end up down here. Tony has so little imagination."

"Who are you?" I was confused and relieved that I appeared to have been rescued by the good guys. We had slowed down and were driving normally through the crowded city streets.

"I'm Hughie Wallsom." I recognised the name, it was on the list that Tash had given me. "We're on the way to the port and you're coming with me – we've got to get you off Centra." There were about a hundred questions in my head. I needed to tell Gaynor what was going on, but somehow I thought that I wouldn't have the chance.

Hughie glanced across at me as we wove through the crowded streets. "Have you managed to get a copy of the drive off of Reevis?"

"Yes I have, Tony here took it off me, just before you arrived." The man holding Tony searched his pockets; finding the drives he passed them back to me.

"Hughie Wallsom, you little shit, you'll suffer for this,"

said Tony as we left the tall buildings of the city behind us and entered the suburbs, residential streets with neat gardens. "I'll see to it."

"That's your trouble, Tony," said Hughie, "you think that you've got all the answers; that you're always right and that Donna will always ride to your rescue. We're onto you now and have the information to blow your operation up."

"I don't think so," he smiled coldly. "You've got nothing. I'm still in control, just let me out and we'll forget all about it." We passed a police car and Tony gazed longingly at it.

"I don't think so," said Hughie. His tone was casual, as if this was the most natural thing in the worlds and he was enjoying it.

"He said he would destroy the dome," I shouted and Hughie nodded. "Oh I know all about that, he's got these delusions of grandeur." Tony scowled at him, wriggling in the grip of the tall man. "Keep him still, Marc, in fact tie him up," said Hughie, "he's about to get a lesson in real power, not the sort that he thinks he has." Marc's considerable arm pinned Tony to the seat.

"Harris Morgan," the man Hughie said casually, "bet you thought you had him where you wanted him. He wasn't worth your attention was he? Well he's one of ours. He stuck around, swallowed his pride, even though you treated him badly. And do you know why?" Tony was silent, but you could see the shock on his face. Mind you, I was shocked to hear what came next.

"Harris didn't like the way you were running the show and not just on Reevis. He was proud of the old Balcom, before your lot corrupted it. He found your little accident waiting to happen, and it won't be having the desired effect. Ever since we first spotted what you were up to, we've been planning to take you down."

Tony slumped into the seat and stopped struggling; all the fight seemed to have gone out of him. "The dome won't rupture?" he muttered softly, repeating it over and over again as it sank in.

"Do you know what your downfall was, Tony?" continued Hughie. Tony was silent.

The man, Marc, gave him a gentle slap on the side of his head with his free hand. "Speak up, Mr Hays," he suggested politely, "Mr Wallsom here can't hear you."

"What?" The smug voice had gone.

"Well I'll tell you then," Hughie continued. "You had a good thing going, you'd made Balcom a front for all sorts of wrongdoing and kept it quiet but it wasn't enough, was it? You got careless, trying to reduce the inspections to save a bit of money. It was unnecessary; it never showed in the accounts so where did the cash go?" Tony was silent. "And do you know, people notice little things like that. And once they spot a scam, they look a little deeper. And it's always the little things that lead to the big things – this time it was the inspector laid off because of the reduced work; his wife works in accounts and notices that no savings are recorded. She then finds something else and it all comes out."

"Little people," said Tony.

"That's right. You don't see them because you think they don't matter, but they do, and that one piece of greed was enough."

It was silent in the car for a few minutes. Marc finished tying Tony's hands together behind his back in a brisk, competent manner and I started to notice our surroundings. We were headed for the Balcom compound, down near the sea. Traffic was light for a weekday, just a few lorries, some with the familiar Balcom logo and the odd car. I had travelled this road many times to the marina. In high summer it was a nightmare, solid with traffic all day.

We reached the entrance to the Balcom plant and stopped at the gate.

"Don't think you can warn anyone," Hughie said, "the gate man is on our side." He opened the window. "Morning, Danny," he said to the uniformed guard.

"Hi, Hughie. Well who have we got there then?" He peered in the window, and seeing the figure of Tony Hays with his hands tied he grinned.

"Oh good," he said, "couldn't happen to a nicer bloke. Good morning, Mr Hays – see, I can remember your name."

"What do you mean?" I asked.

"Well," Danny replied, "he never bothered to learn my name, I was just 'You' to him, no respect for the staff."

"Time to get our company back," said Hughie.

"Yeah," said Danny, "and while we're about it, we want Layla back as well." Hughie shot him a look that I don't think I was meant to see.

It was good to hear her spoken of so fondly; her disappearence was the thing that had got Nic killed and had started me off in this adventure.

"What's that about Layla?" I turned from the window and asked Hughie.

He was evasive. "We all miss her. It would be good to see her again, that's all.

"We were never here, Danny," he said out of the window. Danny nodded, the gate opened and we drove into the facility.

Tony looked totally deflated; he must have thought that he would get away with the assistance of the security guards. Now that he had found that wasn't happening he could see that he had lost.

The Balcom facility was immense; it took at least five minutes to drive past the perimeter fence on the way to the marina, which joined its wharf on one side. That was where I had kept my yacht, the clubhouse where I spent my days, looking over the sea and writing. But there was so much more to it than that, there were several rows of tall warehouses and laboratories, and a large hangar with an airstrip as well as the port facility.

The place was deserted. "It's shut today," said Hughie. "Hyper-drive day." I had forgotten in all the excitement and coming back from Reevis. Balcom gave their workers a day off on the anniversary of the first trans-light flight.

"Donna wanted to stop it of course," Marc growled. "Good day for a getaway."

We arrived at a hangar, there were two craft inside. "These are Balcom executive transports," Hughie told me, "the latest models. We can get to Reevis easily in them, and get Tony stashed somewhere as well."

We all got out of the car and stood by one of the ships. About forty metres long and sleek, they had twin engines on stubby wings and a reputation for luxury inside.

Hughie turned to Tony Hays, who appeared even smaller now that he was bound. "Now, Tony, you are going to stay with a few friends of mine in a place where you will be safe until we can get you arrested." Tony looked down at his feet and said nothing.

"We are going back to Reevis," Hughie said to me. "Donna will follow us looking for Tony here and we can get this mess sorted out."

Hughie and I got into one of the ships while Marc took Tony and put him in the other. "I'll keep him sedated for the trip, Hughie," he said. "I'll be in touch."

The ship had been fuelled and stored by ground crews. "They're kept ready for executives," Hughie explained, "so they can zoom off whenever they want."

I had never seen such opulence in a moving object; it was better than the ocean cruisers on the pleasure planets, all leather and wood panelling. "Is that real marble?" I asked at one point, a phrase I never thought I'd use in a spacecraft. There were five staterooms, cabins for a crew of three, public rooms and stores.

"Pick whichever one you want," said Hughie. "I'm in the pilot's cabin, it's got all the alarms in it." I looked round open-mouthed and chose one of the staterooms. It was better than the room in Nic's hotel, if a little smaller. I had nothing but the clothes I stood up in, but opening the closet showed it full of suits and dresses, in a variety of sizes, together with everything a fugitive on the run might need. "Help yourself," said Hughie, "I'm off to get us moving." He went to the cockpit and in a daze I followed him.

"Strap yourself in," Hughie said. "It won't be as smooth as a shuttle but we'll be fine."

30

Hughie sat at the controls, starting up the engines and talking to the airspace controllers. After checking a long list of settings on a clipboard by the seat he taxied out of the hangar and towards the setting suns. When we swung round and lined up on the runway the other craft was in front of us. As we listened Marc was given clearance to take off. We watched as he lifted into the air and disappeared behind the clouds.

"Our turn now," said Hughie. "Are you ready?" Without waiting for my reply he called and received clearance to take off and we started to roll along the runway. With a sudden burst of acceleration we took off and pointed the needle nose towards the heavens.

My body sank about a foot into the heavily padded seat. "That's like a kick in the back," I gasped. All the air seemed to be trapped in my lungs and I had to force it out to speak. Sitting beside me Hughie was in his element. His eyes scanned the panels for information, the control column steady in his hands.

We went through the clouds and a cover opened on the panel by his knee, revealing a lever. "You think so?" he said. "We're cleared for escape acceleration, try this." He pulled the lever.

I heard the engines howl. My vision blurred and I could feel my head becoming so heavy that I struggled to hold it up. In what seemed like an instant the sky turned black and stars shone. Hughie pushed the lever back down and my arms now lifted back off the seat rests. My weight seemed to have vanished and I realised that we were free of the gravity of Centra. Hughie noticed it too.

"No artificial gravity," he said, "forgot." He pressed a button and everything returned to normal.

He was obviously in his element, despite that slip. "I helped design this ship," he told me, "me and Igor, back when he was still in charge. It has the new engines, improvements all over – it's the future of travel. I haven't flown it for a while but it's coming back to me now just how much I love it."

If Balcom crashed, all this might be lost. "I was thinking," I said, "we will have to be careful not to destroy everything just to get rid of Donna and the Hays."

"You're right," he agreed. "We need a surgical operation, like cutting out a cancer; get all the bad and leave the good bits to regrow."

I thought of what Tash had said. "Do you think that Donna was bad from the day she arrived?"

"Oh yes," he replied, "she had an agenda right from the start. And no one really knows where she came from. One day Igor appeared in the assembly bays for his usual walk around and she was with him. By the speed at which she established a power base and sidelined him, she must have had an organisation behind her."

"Tony told me that Donna put all her enemies in one place, he was quite proud of the fact."

"There's two ways of looking at that," said Hughie. "It's smart to keep your eye on everyone; on Reevis it's a lot easier than in most places. Of course, having them all in one place makes it easier for them to plan as well." Hughie continued, "There's a lot of tension throughout Balcom. Those of us who were here before her feel sidelined, but anyone who complains is seen as a troublemaker."

"Does everyone in Balcom suspect her?" He shook his head.

"No, you have to be high up to see what's going on, it's such a big company. Her activities are spread out and well hidden from most people, but the higher you get the more it can be seen. That's why she has been replacing all the managers with her own men. Anyone who tries to blow the whistle is either sidelined to Reevis or disposed of."

So what she thought was a good idea was really her big mistake, putting all her enemies in one place.

The orbiting customs post gave us clearance to proceed, so we accelerated away from the planet. As soon as we could, we would go to trans-light speed. I was going back to Reevis, but this time it wasn't under false pretences – I knew what I was going to do.

After I had received the familiar kick in the stomach, Hughie and I started talking about a plan. We were sitting in the cockpit, the shutters were up and I was looking at the star map; it looked like a long way back to Reevis.

"We'll be there in no time," said Hughie. "Two days less than the liners take; of course, we don't stop on the way. Donna will guess that's where we are headed. She will have to follow us on a liner."

"Are you sure that she will follow us?"

"Oh yes, she won't leave it to Shelly. They might be sisters but she doesn't trust her that much. If she can't get hold of Tony she will come to sort it out herself."

"Why can't she just use another company ship?"

He laughed. "We have both serviceable ones at the moment and the other one will be unavailable."

"Is that coincidental?" It seemed to me that it was either fortunate or well planned.

"There may be problems with the other one," he replied, straight-faced. "The engineers may not be able to get it space-worthy." The look on his face told me all I needed to know about that. "Just a bit of low level agitation," he said. "Why make things easy for her?"

"What do you think she will do when she gets to Reevis?" I asked him. "She won't be happy to have to chase us, will she?"

"Donna hates Reevis. She will be angry that we have dragged her out there, which makes her more likely to slip up. We won't be able to separate her from her bodyguards and that cow Shelly Hays won't be far away either. Did you see her on Reevis?"

"Yes, I did. I realise now that I was under surveillance by her or Tony most of the time." I told him how Tony was disguised as a policeman with the name that Detective Chumna had got wrong and I told him about the smell of aftershave.

"And you smelt it on the Mayor as well?" he asked.

"In her office. Tony told me just before you rescued me that they were having an affair."

"That would drive Shelly nuts; she's very possessive."

"Shelly seemed a bit crazy to me, telling me she was Harris Morgan's daughter."

"I don't know about that," he said, "but I know that she enjoys playing with people's emotions."

"Harris found it laughable. He said that if she had have been, he would have walloped her."

"Hmm…pity," said Hughie, "that might have saved us all a load of grief."

"Anyhow what's the plan?"

"We'll tell Donna that you have the drive stashed and get her to meet us on the outside of the cluster. Donna will be sure to come for it, especially if she hasn't heard from Tony."

"But the information is on Centra, my editor has it all."

"That's a good backup but on its own it'll never be believed. Donna has so many people on her payroll that the story will never be heard. You must tell your editor that she's not safe if she goes public, tell her to keep it under wraps.

We need to get Donna away from her power base. If we can get her to admit to things and get a record of it, well that would be even better. It would avoid tainting the rest of the company."

"I've told Gaynor, she won't publish 'til I tell her."

"That's good. The trouble is, we're all visible. It's like chess – Donna knows that we will head for Reevis, she'll guess that you're with me and we know that she knows. Everyone will be watching for us to arrive. So we have to be hidden in plain sight. Not only that but we don't know who to trust on Reevis. I've not been there for a while, what do you reckon?"

"I'm fairly sure about Al," I said, "and I've come to see that Harris Morgan is OK."

"I don't know this Al fellow, but Harris is fine; we can rely on him. He's outwardly loyal to her and his personality and reputation carries a lot of the others with him. Shelly doesn't trust him. He adored Layla and is biding his time. Like I said, he knows about the plot to demolish the dome and is neutralising it."

"But he was evil towards me in the diner and in the Mayor's office."

Hughie grinned. "I'll bet Shelly was around in the diner, and the Mayor is a Balcom product, he could hardly tell you it was an act."

"Fair enough, he did come to see me and explain. As for the others, well, they all have an agenda, it's really whether it fits in with ours."

"What about the police?" Hughie asked.

"Difficult to say. I think we need to ask Al before we decide. He's going to be shocked about Harris as well. Changing the subject, how far do you think Donna will be prepared to go?"

"She'll want you dead, and once she finds out I've helped you, me as well. But before she can kill us, she needs to know what we know and who we've told. So having the drive off planet helps as a backup." He asked again, "Your editor will do the sensible thing, right?"

"What's the matter? I've told you she will sit tight until I say; she knows the power of the Balcom PR."

"Sorry to go on about it but she is in danger if she opens her mouth, and I know how keen journalists are to rush off on half a story. We've been planning this for a long time and I don't want it ruined." That annoyed me and I had to respond.

"Then perhaps you should have moved the drive yourselves, and not got me to do it. I'm involved now and I've told you once."

"You're right, of course," he said, "but we couldn't move it off planet ourselves; we were all being watched. When we heard that Nic wanted a review of his hotel we figured that we could use you to take it off planet in your press bag."

I pressed him: "And what do you mean about rushing off, do you mean like me with Layla two years ago?"

He looked puzzled and shook his head. "I don't know much about that; only that Gaynor got you out of prison. She has stuck by you, hasn't she?"

"She's the only one that did. I could understand a lot of people dumping me when I was arrested – in a way they were fair-weather friends, with reputations to protect. But once I was cleared and released, I thought that they would return, but it was like they still believed there was some harm in knowing me. All except her."

"Do you want to tell me about it?"

"I've never really told anyone the full story. Gaynor knows it all but she understands that it's private."

"Well," he said, with devastating logic, "if this all goes wrong I won't be able to pass it on, will I?"

That was a sobering thought, so I decided that perhaps it

was time to open up. "I'll get us a drink, is there somewhere more comfortable we can sit?"

"You're on Igor Balcom's private transport, what do you think?"

We moved out of the cockpit, Hughie carrying a small alarm receiver with him. We sat in the saloon, a room splitting the craft in two. Forward of it were the galley and crew spaces, along with the cockpit. Aft were the staterooms and stores. I went into the small but well equipped galley and made us both a cup of tea. It was real tea as well, not the instant stuff you got on the liners; of course there was a water boiler and proper ceramic cups as well.

We settled ourselves in the deep leather chairs and I began to tell my tale.

31

"Layla had disappeared, and for a gossip columnist that's like Christmas – we can work ourselves up and speculate till our fingers fall off."

Hughie nodded. "But that wasn't your style was it?"

"No, I never met Layla but I respected her. She was a rich kid who had tried to do the right thing. She got an education and didn't just rely on Daddy's cash. And if she wanted a holiday or a tall, dark, handsome lover, well, don't we all want those things?"

"A gossip columnist with a heart," laughed Hughie. "But you're right, I knew her from a child and she was never interested in the money; she paid for all the holidays herself as soon as she could earn, and the clothes were mainly lent by people who wanted the advertising. She knew lots of men, but most were just arm candy, she never had a serious boyfriend that I can remember."

I knew that was true from my research. I took a few sips of tea and carried on.

"She had gone off the social radar a few times before, so when she first went missing no one really took much notice. Then when she didn't turn up where she was expected the gossip started. We dug around and could find no trace of her."

"Neither could we," said Hughie. "I'm with you so far."

I collected my thoughts. "Once we had decided this was more than just her lying low we had an army out looking for her – we all wanted to make sure that the other magazines didn't find her first, so there was a lot of misinformation spread as well. Unsurprisingly there were a lot of runaways that turned up – old man and young girls, forbidden love, that sort of thing. We also found a few kidnappings and then I got a tip-off about a girl being kept in a house on Dalyster."

"That was the best lead yet, wasn't it?" asked Hughie. I nodded.

"It was anonymous, but we had video of a girl who looked like her going into the place. I turned up with a film crew before the police got there and found that the delegate was running an illegal drinking club and brothel, all underage. There were drugs as well, the whole shooting match. It turned out that the police didn't come as they were all in on it but after I published the story the publicity ruined him."

"And Layla wasn't there?"

"No. That was a good thing and a bad thing. At least she wasn't involved, but we still didn't know where she was."

"Igor took it bad, didn't he?"

"Yes. I was so sure that I'd found her that I'd been to tell him. Donna Markes wasn't there but he was pleased. Then when she wasn't there he got angry and accused me of trying to ruin the delegate and extort money from him. It was all lies but with his reputation it stuck."

Hughie laughed. "Sorry, it's not funny but I happen to know that Igor hated the delegate – wasn't he the whiter than white one?"

That was news to me.

"Yes, he had pushed the laws for the protection of children, so it was very embarrassing. Anyway I'm basking in triumph just about to publish my follow-up when the police stop the article, confiscate all my notes and arrest me. The delegate had got his friends to turn it round – suddenly I was running the place and he, the pure delegate, had been set up. It was so laughable that I didn't take it seriously."

"But…" Hughie left it hanging.

"That's right, they all stuck together and the fix was in.

I was tried in a secret court – for the security and anonymity of the minors involved was the official reason. I had no lawyer and couldn't cross-examine. There was no evidence, just the word of a politician against mine. Igor wasn't called to testify that I had been to see him. It was over in five minutes and I got five years."

Hughie shook his head. "So-called justice. Those sort of people always stick together." It sounded like Reevis: out in the crater when anyone was in trouble you stuck together. Only, that was right. What had happened to me was wrong.

"Gaynor wasn't the only one who knew the real story but she was the only one willing to stick her neck out. I don't blame Igor; maybe I shouldn't have got his hopes up. Gaynor fought to clear my name. It took her nearly a year to get enough people to listen to her to get the case reviewed, and in the end I was released. It still nearly went wrong – the shuttle bringing me down from the orbiting prison ship had a problem and a lot of people died. I guess that's where my fear of vacuum comes from."

"Were you on the prison ship?" He looked shocked. "That must have been grim."

"Well let's just say that I came back a changed man and leave it at that."

The orbiting prison ships were old and known to leak. The transfer shuttles were automated death traps. "I was more worried after I knew I was free," I said, "knowing that I could die on my way back to freedom."

32

A day out from Reevis, Hughie called me into the cockpit. "I'm going to try and raise your friend, Al," he told me. "I just hope you're right about him. I don't want to try to talk to Harris, we don't know the situation at Balcom."

"Al will be fine," I said. "Is the call secure?"

"It should be but it doesn't matter anyway," replied Hughie, "I'm not going to use my Balcom codes to route the call, and it's not going through the usual server so it will just look like a tourist enquiry to Al's tours, don't worry."

If he was right and everyone knew we were coming back it shouldn't matter and there was no need to worry. But I couldn't help it.

Hughie punched in the call and after a few seconds it started ringing. In my mind I could see Al's office, with May at the desk. Considering the trouble you sometimes had making a call on Centra, calling an office on a planet from a translight ship with marble fittings was pretty amazing stuff, even to get a dial tone. Hughie passed me the second comm set and I put it on.

"You can talk to him," he said "tell him we will be landing at Dome Twenty."

"Where's that?"

"It's an old research station a fair way from the cluster; he'll know it," he told me. "It's disused, ruined. A meteor strike took out half the roof but it's out of the controlled area so we can land unnoticed. Get him to meet us at fourteen hours local time tomorrow and take us somewhere safe."

May answered our call and I didn't give a name, just

asked for Al Nichols. After a moment Al came on the line. "Hi, it's Miles," I said.

"Hello," he greeted me, "I didn't expect to hear from you so soon."

"Is everything OK down there?" I asked and he thought for a moment, whilst we waited nervously.

"Sure," he said eventually, "I haven't been in the main dome for a couple of days but it's all quiet." I passed him Hughie's message and he agreed to meet us. "Anything else I can do?" he asked.

I looked across at Hughie, who shook his head. "No that's about it, see you tomorrow."

After I disconnected I realised that he didn't know that Harris Morgan was one of the good guys. I wondered how he would take the news. Perhaps I should mention it.

Later we were relaxing in the saloon, after another foray into the executive food stores. I had noticed that a lot of the meals were dome-made.

"These are produced by the farm co-op on Reevis," I said. "I've seen the place; it's impressive."

Hughie put down his fork. "Nothing but the best for the executives," he agreed. "I could get used to this sort of life."

"But you wouldn't let it turn you into a criminal?"

"No," he said with a definite tone, "and I think I'm too soft to wield real power – you have to be a bit ruthless to run a big company like Balcom."

"But from what I recall Igor did it in a good way," I told him. "Everyone respected him and I never heard anyone say he was a bad boss."

"Igor had a talent for spotting everyone's potential and remembering their names. The whole family had the same knack. They inspired people to bring out their best."

"What about Layla?" I asked.

"She had it as well. Everyone thought she would be a brat, her mother was spoiling her and Igor didn't want that. Then there was the accident and she had to grow up fast. In the end Igor's influence was turning her into someone who could follow him."

"Do you think her disappearance had got anything to do with Donna and Tony?"

He gave me a look. "Layla was very critical of both of them; she thought her father was being manipulated and she spoke out. She's well liked by everyone and they would move mountains to protect her. Apart from that, I don't know any more." It seemed to me that he was being evasive; maybe that was because he knew I was a journalist and thought I might use it later.

"I'm switching the alarms to my cabin and getting some sleep," he told me, draining his glass, "busy day tomorrow."

"Before you do," I said, "you do realise that Al doesn't know that Harris is on our side?"

He shrugged. "So?"

"It's more than that," I told him. "Everyone on Reevis thinks that Harris is anti-everything, it's a convincing act. Al's been intimidated by Balcom, we think they nearly killed us when I was there and Al thinks it's Harris pulling the strings."

"We'll just have to convince him then, won't we?" he replied.

The next morning, Reevis's sun was large in the port. We had dropped out of trans-light speed automatically when the star's gravity field had increased and we now coasted in towards the planet at around ninety-five percent light-speed.

"Good morning," Hughie greeted me as I entered the cockpit and sat in the right-hand seat, "have you had breakfast?"

"I thought I'd make my last one a good one so I had the

full pack," I said, wiping bacon fat from my lips with a napkin.

"Get comfy then," he told me, "we'll be coming in shortly."

We could see the planet, or at least the red half of it, out on our port side; we seemed to be flying away from it. "I'm coming in on the dark side and getting low to slip under the customs posts," Hughie explained.

The ship slowly swung towards the red disc and it altered shape into a red crescent as it got larger. We could see the cold side and the ribbon as a shadow that blacked out the stars. When it was huge in our ports the sun disappeared and it all went dark.

We headed straight towards the surface and I watched the readouts from the forward-facing scanner as the distance decreased. The figures changed from hundreds of miles to tens to units then to metres as we closed on the dark expanse of ice. With no atmosphere there was no re-entry as such, we just got closer. I hadn't realised it as there was nothing to reference our motion but we must have been levelling out as the distance stopped at five thousand metres and suddenly a horizon appeared.

"Pretty good automation, though I say it myself," said Hughie with pride and I guessed that the navigation and electronics systems were part of his input into the ship's design.

A ridge of mountains grew larger in front of us, and the ice gave way to grey rock. "That's one of the craters on the ribbon," he explained, "we swing around that and it's only a hop to our crater and the dome."

"Why was the dome that we're going to out here?" I asked Hughie.

"It was a research station," he explained, "the bedrock here was ideal for foundations, and it was far enough away from everything else for secrecy."

We had been slowing all the time, and now we crossed the crater rim and turned, dropping again to a few hundred metres from the ground. I could clearly see a multitude of small craters and boulder fields, and then we climbed over more hills and dropped suddenly into another crater. The navigation computer bleeped.

"Here we are," said Hughie and turned on the lights. Ahead of us was the ruin of a medium-sized dome. At least half of the roof was gone and there were random pieces of equipment scattered around outside it. "No one comes out here," explained Hughie. "I can stash the ship in the dome, it won't be seen." In the distance I could see a line of yellow flashing markers. "That's the lower rim road," he said.

As we swooped under the cliffs, there was a splash of colour in the grey gloom below as an EV turned its lights on. "That'll be Al," I said, "his EVs are all yellow like that."

Hughie piloted the ship in through the hole and landed under the remains of the roof. "As long as it doesn't fall in we'll be fine," he said. As he shut down I got into a suit and Hughie followed. I felt surprised that it didn't bother me anymore.

Al had brought his EV in through the old lock, now wedged open. We left the ship and walked across to him through powdered soil that threw up puffs of dust. Surprisingly there were still mosses flourishing on the last of the nutrients. We got into the EV and the lock hissed shut behind us. "Hi, everyone," said Al as we took off our helmets and settled into the seats. "You must be Hughie, welcome to Reevis. Good trip?"

Hughie shook his hand. "Hello, Al. I've been here before but not for a while. Miles here says I can trust you."

"You can at that," replied Al. "I'm no fan of the Hays and I've a good idea of what's going on here." You just wait, I thought to myself.

Hughie filled him in on the events on Centra, and then Al had a few bits of information of his own to add.

"Donna is due; she's arriving tomorrow, and she had to come on a liner. Someone," and he looked at us, "had taken both her company transports."

"I wonder who that could have been," chuckled Hughie innocently. "We only had one. Tony must have taken the other."

"I've got a safe place for you," said Al, "you've been there before, Miles." I assumed that he meant the farm as we set off through the ruined lock and headed out in a wide sweep around the cliffs. This brought us back towards the line of flashing posts marking the road around the crater. Far away I could see the Ugly Sisters shining in the perpetual sunlight and off to my left the lights of the cluster. It felt like looking at trouble, coming to meet me.

"Now it looks like we have come from the ice field," said Al, "and we can head off to the lookout." So we weren't going back to the farm, which suited me perfectly well.

He called Dome Control: "Alpha Tango Zero One, we are re-entering your controlled area, and I'm heading for the look-out to drop supplies." They acknowledged as we bounced over the grey dust towards the yellow marker. "It's the truth," he said, "I've got a load of ice on the back."

After about an hour moving across the featureless plain we climbed up the ramp onto the rim road, and in no time we were in the lookout. After we had got out Al manoeuvred the EV till it was under a small crane that folded out from the rock wall. He used it to unload the ice, which was swung into a chute. "That'll be crushed and separated," he said. "There's enough oxygen in there for a few weeks." He also told us that he had brought food up with him and we unloaded the boxes. So we were self-sufficient for a couple of weeks. He had also left an EV there, in case we needed to move out.

Over a meal we discussed our next move. I thought that the whole situation was getting too big for a bunch of amateurs to handle. "Can we trust anyone in the Reevis City Police?" Hughie asked Al.

He was silent for a moment, savouring the beef and vegetables. "Probably Flanagan," he answered, "he seems fairly honest, but it would have to be without his partner."

I nodded, "Tash said the same."

"But isn't this Tash the one who goes off for months at a time prospecting?" Hughie asked. "She can't be here long enough to see all that goes on."

Al got upset at that. "Neither are you, chum, but we're listening to your opinions. Tash might be out exploring a lot but at least she's on the planet, and she keeps in touch."

"OK, sorry," said Hughie, "point taken. Flanagan then."

"I can get in touch with him and get him up here," said Al, still obviously annoyed with the dismissal of Tash. I was a bit upset too; after all, she had saved my life and I thought more of her than I cared to admit. Then, to add to the tension, Hughie dropped the bomb.

"We have Harris," said Hughie, "and he's—"

Al exploded, "Oh no, not him. I won't have anything to do with that man, he's been on my case for too long."

"Listen," said Hughie, "it's all an act, Harris is on—"

But Al shouted him down: "No! I'll go along with the idea of Balcom being crooked, but not with Harris Morgan being some kind of double agent."

I felt like I had to speak up. "Al, do you trust me?"

He looked at me, "Yes," he said after a pause, "I reckon I do. What do you think about this rubbish?"

"When I left last time, Harris spoke to me; he told me he was really working against the Hays." Al looked very dubious.

"But everyone knows Harris is behind all the intimidation."

"Flanagan told me it couldn't be proved."

"Well, I'm still not convinced." Al resumed eating and kept his face down, shovelling the food in as if it had insulted him. There was silence until he lifted his head. Then Al and Hughie glared at each other. I tried to act as peacemaker.

"This isn't getting us anywhere – agree to disagree if you must, just leave Harris out of it for now if it keeps us moving. What's next?"

"Then we need to get Donna somewhere," Hughie continued, "separate her from her bodyguards and get her to admit everything that's been going on."

Al looked at him. "Dead easy then," he said sarcastically. "How do you suggest we do that, ask nicely?"

This was getting silly. Clearly Al and Hughie were never going to be best buddies but for the sake of our plan they had to get along.

"Listen, you two," I shouted, "you don't have to get on but you can at least agree on a plan. Hughie's right, all we need to do is get her somewhere she feels safe and in control, where she feels like she can say anything without comeback."

"Fair enough," said Al. "If she thinks you're dead anyway, she won't be able to resist bragging."

"Exactly," agreed Hughie.

"So we need to be in an apparently helpless position," I said, "at her mercy, and she'll spill the beans."

"That's right," said Hughie, "all we need to do is work out how to survive with the admission."

"Let's speak to Flanagan about that."

"I'll go and get him tomorrow then," said Al. Hughie just grunted and went to sit in one of the EVs. This was all we needed. Never mind Balcom; we were busy fighting each other.

33

Al must have left really early morning as he was gone by the time Hughie and I had got up. We breakfasted watching the lava boil, seeing the skimmers drift over the surface and gazing at the unblinking star. Hughie was as enraptured with the sight as I was. "People would pay to have holiday homes here," he said. "Your friend Nic had the right idea."

"He wasn't really my friend," I said. "Gaynor knew him but I never met him until I saw his body in my bathroom, but you're right. And the only reason that this place is not a pleasure planet is Balcom. If they were an honest company the whole place would open up." He agreed with me, "You're right, of course, and if we can weed out all the bad then maybe we can do just that."

I told him the thoughts that I had had, of the string of places like this that could be built in the cliffs, a series of self-contained holiday villas, all sharing the view yet being cut off from each other, with fine food and drink from the farm and high service levels. He was enthusiastic about the concept. "You know, you should tender for the job," he said, "you've got a good business plan there."

Al arrived back in the late afternoon. I was a bit anxious to see him arrive. I had found Hughie easy to get on with; a bit quieter than Al, but just as dependable. I thought from the way they had bristled at each other last night that there might be some tension but Hughie reassured me on that.

"It takes me a while to get to know someone," he explained. "I'm really only starting to trust you now. What will happen

205

here is so important to so many people that I can't afford to risk it."

I could understand that.

"And you have to admit," he continued, "finding out about Harris was bound to be a bit of a shock." That was also true; it had shocked me at the time.

When Al came through the airlock and opened the EV, Flanagan came out with him. He still had the same crumpled suit on but he shook my hand. "I thought you'd be back," he said.

"I need your help," I replied and he smiled. "This is Hughie Wallsom, from Balcom on Centra," I said. "We all need to listen to him." I introduced him and they shook hands.

"So this is the conspiracy," he announced. "I thought there would be more of us." The significance of that remark was not lost on me.

Hughie asked him if he would act to protect us against Donna and Shelly. We hadn't considered what we would do if he said no, but to our relief he agreed.

"The law says that I must, and that's my job," he replied. "You can tell by the suit that I'm not a rich man but I'm honest, I'm not in anyone's pocket. I'm single so there's no lever anyone could have on me. People think that I'm stupid not to take the bribes and look the other way, but that's not what I promised. I think they're the stupid ones."

We all sat facing the lava and Flanagan gave us some news.

"Donna Markes has arrived," he said, "and she's not happy. She's looking for Hughie and Tony; your name was mentioned as well."

Hughie laughed. "Well Tony's light years away, never mind where."

"By the way," said Al, a bit sheepishly, "before we get started, I saw Harris Morgan in town."

"And?" Hughie and I said together.

"He started shouting at me, but I managed to get him in a quiet place and asked him if he had been responsible for driving me and Miles off the ramp." I remembered the rig coming towards us and shuddered.

"What did he say?"

"He said that he didn't, but I told him that I found that hard to believe. He said that he was glad that Tash had rescued us. I asked him how he knew that and he said that she had told him."

"So does that alter your opinion?" Hughie was first with the question. "I'll have to meet this Tash; seems I was a bit hasty about her yesterday."

"Well if Tash and Harris are on speaking terms," said Al, "then clearly there's more to him than the goon image. So I asked him straight, are you a fan of Tony Hays."

"What happened then?"

"Then I thought he *would* hit me. He got quite emotional about the state of Balcom and I did start to believe him. He's got to get credit for that; he's had me and most people here fooled for a long while."

This was progress. Everyone was getting on the same side at last – now maybe we could move forward.

"He said one last thing," said Al. "He asked me if I had Miles with me on Reevis and I said that I did. Then he said that Miles was vital to the future of Reevis, and of Balcom, and that he would never order or encourage any harm to befall him."

Flanagan had been listening to this with obvious disbelief. "Wait a minute," he eventually said, "are you telling me that Harris Morgan is part of all this?"

Here we go again, I thought to myself.

Al looked at Flanagan. "Have you any evidence that Harris Morgan is committing crimes on Reevis?"

"No, like I told Miles before, we can't link any of it back to him." It looked like Harris was gaining a lot of friends.

Between us we filled Flanagan in on our plan to get Donna to admit to her wrongdoing.

"We need her to tell us that we're right about her and we need to record it."

"We can record the conversation in our EV," said Al, "if we go to a private channel."

"Then all we have to do is survive."

Flanagan agreed with our strategy. "If you tell me when and where, I can be just around the corner in a police car."

"Can you organise that without alerting any of Tony's tame policemen?" Hughie asked.

"Oh yes, I know who they are. It'll be easier at the moment," he said, "Chummie's disappeared, about the same time that Donna arrived." I remembered that Tash hadn't liked him. Flanagan continued, "I've never trusted him; he was a bit vague about the tip-off that brought us to your room that night, and he always had loads of cash but I could never work out where it came from."

"Sounds to me like he was on someone's payroll then."

"Yes and it's helpful that he's not around, that's one that I won't have to share any of this with."

We talked through a few more ideas. Flanagan said he would give us a police radio so that he could listen in. "I can record from it as well and then when I have enough to work with I can come in and rescue you."

"Don't leave it too long, please," I said. "She's not going to leave us alive to tell the tale."

"It's a good plan," he agreed. "Don't worry, you'll be quite safe."

"So all we need to do is get Donna outside," said Hughie. "She has two bodyguards with her at all times; they will be in separate vehicles to cover her, probably a Doris with a drill

– that would take care of most EVs, maybe a few explosive charges as well."

"I can go and arrange the meeting," offered Hughie. Al and I could see the problems there.

"It's too dangerous for you to go, Hughie," Al voiced it. "She'll realise that it's a set-up."

"I don't think so," was his calm answer. "Look. Tony hasn't been able to pass on any information to her, she'll be wondering where he is. The last she knew, I wasn't involved, it was just Tony in the car park getting rid of Miles here. If I turn up and say that I found you on Centra and managed to get you here, she'll be relieved and angry that Tony messed up."

"Sounds good so far," said Flanagan, "go on, Hughie."

"If I tell Donna you've got the drive and that you trust me she may fall for the idea of a meeting to get it back. She's going to kill you anyway – out in the open she will feel safe to do it."

"Yes but what about your safety?" It seemed unnecessarily risky to me but there wasn't any real choice.

"I'm not under suspicion yet," he said, "but the important thing is getting her out of circulation and getting Balcom returned to its rightful owners." That was true and I felt respect for Hughie and his selfless efforts.

"Changing the subject," I asked, "have we heard from Tash, Al?"

"No but both me and Harris have left messages all over the planet for her, and as far as we know she's safe."

In the end you couldn't argue with Hughie's logic, so he went back to the farm with Al and Flanagan to start to spread the word, leaving me alone in the lookout. I had no way of communicating with them and didn't know how long they would be. At least they left me some beer and food.

34

Left on my own there was little I could do except watch the lava field below me and think up plans for a future on Reevis. I was pretty sure that this was where I wanted to spend the rest of my life, and I was also pretty sure who I wanted to spend it with.

I could probably get a job with Al, or even go prospecting; the place had got a hold over me with its beauty, or was it just the thought of being with Tash? The days passed slowly as I tried not to worry about what was going on.

On the third day, I was just walking around the look-out trying to keep active when I saw the lights of a vehicle coming down the canyon towards the airlock. It was probably Al returning but I had sudden thoughts that Shelly or Donna had come to get me. Perhaps Al and Hughie had been grabbed and interrogated, the whole plan had collapsed – my mind was doing somersaults as I raced into the EV and shut the hatch.

I was desperately trying to remember how to start the engines when the source of the lights arrived at the airlock. It wasn't Al's EV, nor was it a police rig. The outer door opened and it came in. The lock started to pressurise. It was a tug unit, I recognised the general shape from others I had seen; they towed heavy ore trailers around and drilling platforms or accommodation units. This one had a purple stripe diagonally across the front. Large and powerful it was unencumbered by a trailer and probably more than a match for my EV. I couldn't get past it anyway; it was too wide and only just fitted in the lock.

The inner door opened and it came into the lookout. The engine ran down with a puff of smoke from the exhaust. I was still fiddling with the start-up sequence, trying to remember how Al had done it. At least I had secured the door; whoever it was wouldn't be able to get in here easily. I looked at the door as it opened.

Tash climbed down. "Hey, Miles, where are you?" she shouted.

I jumped off my seat and out of the EV. Running towards each other we met and I swept her up in my arms, she lifted her feet off the ground and I swung her around. We kissed deeply, oblivious to everything else. She was wearing her black boiler suit and her hair was escaping from under a cap; the fringe was almost in her eyes and the peak kept bumping my forehead.

Reluctantly we parted. Still holding onto each other we spoke at once, "It's so good to see you. How long have you been here? What's happening? I missed you." Who said what and in what order I couldn't say.

"I couldn't stop thinking about you," she told me after we finally calmed down and sat together facing the glass. "I just found out you were back."

"I've missed you so much," I told her. "Your note was the worst thing about my last time here. It made me realise how much I didn't want you to go, even though I'd just met you."

She smiled. "Me too, and after I'd sneaked out I realised it too. I kept moving away because I didn't want to believe it. Then when I heard that Hughie was in the dome, I knew that you'd be around somewhere."

I told her the plan, and that Hughie was in town getting it organised. "Of course I'll help," she agreed, "it'll be fun to spoil Donna's day. And you'll know it's me," she pointed to the front of her Tug, "my rig is easy to spot."

All I would have to do would be to get her a message about the meeting when we knew.

We ate. I found the best bits of the food stores and a bottle of wine, dome-made of course, and she dimmed all the lights in the lookout. "I want to see the lava properly," she told me. The result was deep shadow and at times I could hardly make out her face. We talked for hours about our lives and feelings for each other, and I think we could both see where this was leading us.

She had plans for the future as well. "I want to go deep into the ice," she said. We were sitting in one of the armchairs, well I was sitting and she was sitting on me. "Far away from here, take a long time and look at everything – there's a whole planet to discover."

"Is there room for two?" I asked. "It sounds like fun."

"If you don't mind squeezing up," she laughed. I assured her that it wouldn't be a problem.

"I just want to get away from all the hassle," she said, "all the moaning and petty squabbling." I could agree with that.

"Once this is all over, I'd be honoured to come with you." I almost said 'my love' but stopped myself; I didn't want to spoil the moment.

She saved me the bother. "Would you think I was being silly if I said that I was falling for you?" She said it in a whisper, as if frightened to admit it. Her dark eyes were like saucers as she looked into mine.

Time stood still as I said it. She smiled and rose, walking to the utility space, where the bunks were. "Come with me."

Again, she wouldn't let me see her as we got into bed; all the lights were off in the sleeping quarters and I banged my knees and elbows continually in the dark as I blundered around in the unfamiliar setting, trying to find her by the sound of her laughter.

35

The night was better than the first one but, again, she wasn't there when I woke. I had a sudden lurch of panic – surely she hadn't left me again? – and then I heard her in the galley. She was singing an old lullaby, something I hadn't heard since my childhood on Centra.

We had breakfast together and she reluctantly left. She said she would be waiting to hear about the meeting and not to worry. For once in my recent life I actually felt like things were moving in the right direction as I waved her away.

The next day, Al came back. "I saw Hughie the day before yesterday. He told me that he went to see Shelly, and that Donna was with her," he said, "and he called me yesterday morning to say when and where we were meeting but I haven't seen him since."

"So Donna went for it then?" I was relieved. I wondered if maybe she wouldn't bother and just try to destroy the dome anyway.

"Hughie said she told him she was scared of what you'd learned and needed to see you herself – she wants the drive. She was getting so agitated at Tony's losing you that she let slip that after she had the drive you were expendable."

"How did Hughie explain me being here?"

"He spun her some story about how you had got away from Tony in the car park and bumped into him while you were running away. He told her that he had managed to persuade you that he would keep you safe and decided that it would be best to bring you here, where you could be controlled."

It was so close to the truth that it sounded plausible. Still, Hughie was on very thin ice; one slip and it would all be over for him.

"Hughie even apologised for taking the ship but said that the other one was still there when he left." Al laughed at that. "Do you know what Hughie told me?" he said. "She actually thanked him and said that a bonus would be on the way."

"You said you have the place and time. Where is it?" I asked, as if it would mean anything to me. But I was thinking it would be nice to see my potential final resting place.

"It's off the mapping in the south of the crater, right out in the sticks; there are just a few ore carriers that use that section of the road."

"Is there an escape route?" I needed to know.

"Don't worry," he said, "I've spoken to Flanagan. That's why I took the extra day, he was busy. He will stake the place out and rescue us before it all goes wrong." He still looked worried, so I asked him what was up.

"I've left messages everywhere for Tash," Al told me. "No one's seen or heard from her for ages."

"It's OK, she was here yesterday," I said and his face lit up. "She's safe then."

"She heard about Hughie being in the dome," I told him, "she reckoned it must mean that I was back and she guessed I'd be hiding out up here."

"Hughie told me yesterday that all the Balcom staff have to attend a meeting in one of the research domes tomorrow afternoon."

That sounded ominous. "Do you think it's connected with our meeting?"

"Well it's all staff, not just the ones on shift, and as it's straight after she intends to deal with you I'd say it looks like Donna is tidying up."

*

214

Al had brought some fresh supplies up from the farm, including an enormous side of salmon, which he dressed and steamed with salads and new potatoes. After clearing the table he spread out a large map of the crater and showed me what was going to happen.

The crater was drawn about two metres across and a lot of the detail, especially on the far side from the cluster, was vague. Roads were marked in the same colour dots as the beacons, and the cluster looked very insignificant in one corner.

"We're here," Al pointed to a small dot in the cliff face, labelled 'Lookout', "and this is the rim road," again a line of dots. "That's the ramp we fell off." I was getting the hang of the markings and followed his pointing with some of my own.

"That must be the old dome where we landed then."

"You got it," he nodded. "Now here," and he indicated a spot on the crater floor well removed from most of the other markings, "is where we have to be tomorrow at noon."

"Donna has a sense of melodrama," I said. "High Noon indeed."

"That's right; I guess she sees it as the traditional time to vanquish all your enemies. You can see it's a route marker on the road, Post 37. Now we can lie somewhere under the cliffs so we're safe from the rear and there is an old up ramp just to the south of it. That means we can get back here the other way around the rim if we have to make a run for it."

"It's quite a way to run, and if someone's chasing you they might have reinforcements as well."

"That's true, but we have to rely on Flanagan to round them up. We will have to leave early tomorrow morning and we have some work to do on the EV first."

Al had come back in one of his larger EVs this time, a twelve-seater. "We'll take this EV," he said, "it's got a bigger engine; we just need to strip the seats out and put extra oxygen tanks in."

"You could have done this in your workshop," I told him, as we manhandled the heavy stuff around.

"Yes, but May would have got wind of what was happening," he said sheepishly. "I love her to bits but she can go on sometimes; she'd want to come with us and I don't want her put in danger." In the past I had envied him his happiness with May, now I could almost touch it for myself.

Flanagan had given him a receiver tuned to police frequencies with a recorder. He mounted it on the dashboard and linked it into the EV's comms gear. "Now it will transmit what we say and hear on the other radio, and record it as well," he said.

In the end we hardly slept and made an early start. Al decided to drive to Post 37 the same way we would be coming back if we had to run for it. "I haven't been along that section of the rim road for a while," he said, "and there may have been changes, maybe rock falls or debris, that sort of thing. It's outside Dome Control so there's no traffic updates."

He drove, but explained all the controls to me first; it was the same as the smaller EV but had a lot more power and acceleration, especially now that it had been lightened. I reckoned I could control it at a push.

The rim road was a lot less defined in this section, clearly it was quieter. "There's not a lot round here," Al told me, "and now that a flat route has been surveyed into the ice the big transports find that easier."

There were a couple of rock falls that restricted the width and a lot more gaps in the cliffs; in places the lava sea was little more than a hundred metres away. There were beaches of sand and pebbles, with lava waves breaking on them. A couple of the places looked like prime sites for hotels. I told Al about my ideas. "Nic thought the same," he said, with a sad note in his voice. "It would be nice to finish what he started."

36

We passed the up ramp, again it looked deserted. I suggested reversing down it to take a look but Al was against the idea. "If we had mapping I might," he said, "but I'd rather not. We have time so we'll go around." We drove on for a while and found the down ramp. We got down without incident and raced along the floor of the crater. Al planned to go to the up ramp and circle round. It was a short hop to the ramp and we climbed quickly back up. This ramp was narrow and had tight turns. "It was built before the super-sized ore trailers came out," he said, "they can't get up here." I wondered if Tash's rig could make it up here. "It might struggle on some of the corners," said Al, "but her rig isn't one of the huge ones. Remember she navigates the ice fields and the gaps are a lot smaller there."

After completing the circle we approached Post 37, passing a rest stop filled with ore carriers and drilling rigs, clustered around in a bunch. It was an hour before noon.

"Here we are, Post 37," said Al. "We're early, there's no one here." Opposite the post was a gully, wide and shallow. "We'll go in there and turn," said Al, "then our rear is covered." Al got us into position and shut the lights down, leaving the engine idling. We faced the post but were protected to the rear and sides from anyone trying to sneak up on us.

With about half an hour to go Flanagan called us on the police radio. He had arrived with two extra unmarked EVs; they were hiding out a short distance away, in the shadow of the cliffs and were listening out.

Tension mounted in the EV as the time approached.

After we had checked that Flanagan was listening and recording there was nothing to do but wait, so we sat in silence, alone with our thoughts. All I could think of was Tash. We had left messages about the meeting place everywhere. Al had spoken to Harris in town and he was also trying to contact her but nothing had been heard, so we didn't know if she would be here.

Traffic was light, just the occasional ore carrier. The mapping was at the edge of coverage from the control room – no doubt that was why this place was chosen. A convoy of transports rolled past, obscuring the view of the flashing post; when they cleared we were not alone.

A large Multi sat on the other side of the post; its lights came on and we were illuminated in the glare. Al flicked our lights on and we tried to out-dazzle each other.

As we faced each other across the road Donna's voice came over the radio. "So, Mr Goram, it would appear I have you where I want you, and now we can finally put this matter to rest. My friends will stop you from leaving."

There was motion to my left and a small vehicle appeared: it was a Doris with a drill rotating on its jib, which poked out flat like a lance. Al tapped my shoulder; I could also see a similar vehicle coming from the right.

"I see my two guards have turned up," said Donna. "Before we complete our business there are a few things you need to know."

Al and I looked at each other realising that we were running out of options – we needed to get her admission. "Go on then," I said.

"Where to start," she replied, her voice sounding calm and triumphant. "Ah yes, firstly, I've been looking for Ms Balcom for quite some time but I never thought I would find her here, with your help."

"What on earth do you mean?" I replied.

She laughed. "Haven't you worked it out yet?"

Another voice came over the radio and I recognised it as Detective Chumna. "Really, Mr Goram, sometimes I despair of people; it was so easy to keep an eye on you."

"Chumna. You're working for her!" I shouted it out and then he laughed as well.

"Well done, Mr Goram, you took your time. Of course I am, how do you think we were able to keep up with you? Even with all your attempts to shake us off it was just too easy."

"Did you kill Nic?"

"Yes, that was me. Shelly told me that Nic had the drive. I knew you would be delayed, but I called him over to that hotel room, knowing he would be expecting you. Of course he had never heard your voice so it was easy to be you. I arrived after him, we argued and I killed him. But I never found the drive. It was easy to pretend to get a tip-off and come back to find the body – of course I had to fool Flanagan, but I'd been doing that for some time anyway. Where was the drive, as a matter of interest?"

"It was in his jacket, so that's why my room was burgled."

"You had to have found it. Tony wanted it back. We knew it would be a copy but once we could see what you had we could start to discredit it."

"But by the time you got the jacket back, I had already got it."

"That's right."

"But what you didn't know was, it wasn't the drive you were expecting, it was a story about Layla Balcom."

He sounded shocked, "Why does everyone always go on about Layla Balcom?"

"Shut up, Chumna," said Donna. "I don't care about Layla, I'm more interested in the files."

"What files?" I wanted to get her on record and felt the

conversation was drifting. Flanagan didn't have anything on Donna; Chumna had admitted to murder but Flanagan wouldn't come to our rescue yet.

"You told me back on Centra that you have some confidential Balcom files," she responded. "Since you have no doubt seen them, perhaps you can tell me what they are about."

"The way you've taken over Balcom to hide your criminal activities. And the way you've hidden under its reputation. Not to mention the compromising of the safety of the dome."

"Oh please, you have no proof, just a few silly letters and memos that could mean anything."

"Tony has told me what you mean to do. People will die, your sister maybe."

"How melodramatic. But to put your mind at rest, she's long gone. Which reminds me, I haven't seen Tony for a while – since your paths crossed on Centra to be exact. Shelly was quite concerned. Where is he?"

"He's quite safe. Has he told Shelly about him and the Mayor?" There was silence for a moment. She still hadn't said anything incriminating; the drills on the Dorises rotated blocking our escape and time was surely running out.

Donna spoke again, "Shelly will get over it, and sometimes you need to do things to keep the plan in motion. Which reminds me, I have someone here, so perhaps we can trade."

My heart skipped – did they have Tash? I hadn't seen her for two days and no one had heard from her.

"I'm listening."

"We have Mr Wallsom here." I felt relieved that it wasn't Tash, but sad because I liked Hughie and he had been a real help to me, plus he had been brave enough to get into the situation, knowing the risks.

"If you bring the drive over to me you can return with him and we will all go our separate ways." Her voice was very persuasive and I almost believed her.

"Don't do it, Miles," shouted Hughie. His words were followed by a thud and a groan.

"Mr Wallsom was speaking out of turn," said a slightly breathless Donna, her calm façade cracking. "Now bring me the drive and we can end this unpleasantness."

Beside me Al turned off the mic. "Hughie is right, we don't deal."

"I can't do that," I said, turning the mic back on, "you're going to kill us all whether I give you the drive or not, like you said, it's a copy. I just want to hear you say it's all true – if I'm going to die then give me the truth."

"So what if it is? You'll never be able to prove it and you'll take it to your death. Yes, it's all true. I took over Balcom to hide my criminal activities, and I'll destroy the dome to hide them. We all have a boss, Mr Goram, and mine is relying on me keeping the money tree growing. Mr Wallsom will be paying the same price that you will just as soon as we have sorted you out."

Hopefully Flanagan had got all that. Surely now he could come to our rescue.

There was the occasional passing vehicle on the road and I realised that their presence was keeping us safe.

"I think that concludes our business," said Donna. "My friends with the drills are just waiting for my command when there's a gap in the traffic."

Al and I exchanged glances – it looked like it was all over. Al winked at me and pointed to the EV's controls. I could see that the reverse gear was engaged, and he was holding the EV on the brakes. He rattled his seatbelt and I understood his meaning and checked my straps. Where the hell was Flanagan?

37

While we had been talking, the two Dorises had been slowly approaching, their drills rotating. They stopped about ten metres from us, one on each side. There was a small gap between the rock and the Doris on the right, maybe we could squeeze through, but not from a standing start.

"That drill can cut through rock," said Al, "our hull would be no problem. Put your visor down."

"That's just prolonging the agony; they will run us down if we climb out."

Where was Flanagan?

"I think that our conversation is at an end," said Donna.

"Wait, just one more thing. You said that I led you to Layla; how did I do that?"

She laughed. "You really can't see it, can you? Goodbye, Mr Goram."

We had limited room behind us, maybe enough to back up a bit; it would give us a couple of seconds at best. Then I understood what Al was up to.

As the Doris on our left lurched forward, Al floored the gas and released the brakes. We shot backwards and hit the rock with a crash that stretched my seatbelt and rattled my teeth. Al had spun the steering as we reversed and we had started to turn away from the drill on our left. Now they both came towards us. Al spun the wheel the other way, selected forward gear and we were away. There was a grinding noise from the rear of our EV as we accelerated, and one of the drills slid down our side; the tip screeched as we fishtailed past but it didn't catch in the metal. We just made it through the gap between the rocks and the Doris and bounced onto the roadway. The rear was sliding from side to side as the automation tried to stop us from flipping over.

I called Flanagan on the secure police radio. "We got away," I told him.

"OK," he answered, "we have enough recorded, and we are moving in to round them up." He had been waiting just around the corner with reinforcements; now he moved in and I could see flashing blue lights in my mirror, through the smoke from our rear. They were joined by red lights on our dashboard.

"We damaged a wheel bearing hitting the cliff," said Al. "Donna's chasing us."

Donna was about a hundred metres behind us. Her larger Multi had lower acceleration but a higher top speed and it would only be a matter of time till she caught us. And we could see that she had explosive charges fitted in a launcher. Al kept the power on and we wove in and out of the light traffic on the way to the up ramp, smoke billowing from our rear.

Donna was gradually catching us up, cutting corners and ignoring the marked route. We entered a debris field, forcing her to stick to the markers but now she was only fifty metres behind. We passed the rest stop, still filled with rigs, one of which looked familiar. I thought I saw a purple stripe. "Isn't that Tash?" I shouted but Al was too busy fighting for control to notice.

The rig, with a wide trailer festooned with gear, pulled out right behind us, forcing Donna to slow. There was no way she could overtake; traffic was coming the other way and Tash's manoeuvre had blocked Donna from catching us.

The ramp was approaching. As I had thought, it was really only wide enough for Tash, so Donna could not get past until we were up. Tash slowed and weaved from side to side to give us a start but we were limping now. One wheel had practically locked up and Al was sweating at the controls as he tried to keep us from the edge.

We could hear Flanagan; he had brought the police to the scene and had Donna's two henchmen in custody. "Flanagan," I called him, "we are on the up ramp with Donna in pursuit. We are damaged and limping, we need your help."

"I'll leave my boys to tidy up, I'm coming after you."

The drop looked big from the corners as we gained altitude. We could see Tash and Donna below us on the climbs. I looked back and couldn't see Flanagan or any other traffic.

Eventually we reached level ground and started along the rim road, heading for the lookout. We were on the cliff side and as we moved past the gaps, bright light shone on us. The grinding was getting louder and Al gave up on the steering, locking it full on, which was just about keeping us level. Fortunately there was a long straight ahead of us. Tash called on the radio, "I'm up and weaving around to stop her passing."

"Well done, Tash," Al called, "but we have a problem – we've got a damaged axle."

"I can see the smoke," said Tash. Her voice sounded excited over the radio. "Have you lost control?"

"Pretty much," replied Al.

"OK," she said, "I will come up close behind. You'll have to jump across, before we get to the curve."

It wouldn't take her long; she was gaining on us rapidly as we approached a curve in the road. Our speed had dropped to a crawl.

With the wheel hard over and the edge of the road approaching we had nowhere to go. Al flipped his visor closed and tapped me on the shoulder. "Come on then."

I did the same and followed him as he left his seat and moved to the back of the cabin. We entered the lock. I knew that the edge was getting closer and was glad to be distracted. Al didn't bother with the lock, just hit the emergency release and the pressure blew the door away.

I could see Tash about three metres behind us, the access platform on the front of her rig bobbing just out of reach. The EV lurched and Al took his chance. He leapt across the gap, landing on the platform of her Tug. He clipped his safety line to the railing and turned, waving me forward.

I looked down. The ground wasn't much of a blur as we were moving slower now, and to my left the wheel was glowing red as the metal ground against itself. The EV started to tip over the edge as I jumped. My last thought was that I had missed as Tash swung right to keep on the road.

I came round in the cab. Tash and Al were talking to me, and my suit helmet was off. My head throbbed. We were still bouncing along but Donna was close behind, trying to get past.

There was a spurt of flame past our left window.

"She's trying to get a clear shot with her drilling charges," said Tash. "She's only got two, but if she hits a wheel we're in trouble." The charge hit the ground in front of us and exploded, making a crater which Tash had to haul the rig around. She got the tractor past safely but one wheel of the trailer dropped into the hole. The chassis of the unit dragged along the ground until the wheel popped out. We had slowed but were still mobile.

"You OK?" asked Al. "You left it a bit late and I had to grab you. You swung around a bit and cracked your visor." He pointed to my helmet; the faceplate was cracked in several places. "Luckily there was enough atmo in the tank to keep you going till I got you inside."

Tash grinned. "Hi, Miles, this beats drilling for samples, much more exciting. Sorry it's a bit cramped in here, it's only really meant for two."

"That's OK, I like cosy," I said, my voice sounding remarkably calm, considering. "We didn't know if you'd got the message. That's two I owe you."

She had a skullcap on, and in the harsh lights of the cab and without the hair her face looked familiar. "Harris told me, I might have to take you up on that," she replied with a grin.

"What are we going to do about Donna? Persistent, isn't she?" Al brought us back to the moment.

Donna fired the second of the charges; it hit the side of the trailer and bounced off without exploding. "Bad fuse," shouted Tash. It bounced over the ground and Donna drove past it just as it went off. The force of the blast lifted her Multi off the ground but it stayed upright and kept coming.

Flanagan's voice came over the radio: "Donna Markes, this is the Reevis City Police. Stop your Multi immediately." Her response was to try and slide between us and the cliff wall.

Tash swung the trailer and she backed off. We were getting near to the site of Al's lookout and the cliff wall had lots of gaps in it. In desperation Donna swung right and as we countered raced left. She was level with the trailer almost before Tash could react; she swung the wheel and hit the trailer release.

The trailer started to slew sideways as it detached and it caught Donna's Multi, tangling in the wheels. We were level with a gap, with a ten-metre drop to a shelving gravel beach, studded with rocks.

38

As we pulled to a halt we watched in the mirrors and through the rear window as the tangle of vehicles slid towards the gap. The weight of the trailer and its momentum pushed the Multi over the edge. The trailer tipped up as gravity dragged it over and it disappeared.

Relieved of the weight our Tug had stopped quickly and Tash turned it around. We headed back to the gap and got there just as a police car arrived, lights flashing. We both got as close to the edge as we could and watched the scene below.

Donna was revving her Multi, the wheels throwing up clouds of cherry-red dust as she fought to break free of the trailer. But the weight was too much for her Multi to overcome and slowly, bathed in red light, the trailer slid down the slope, dragging the Multi with it. It had clearly been hit by the falling trailer as the roof was dented and crumpled.

The cliff sloped gently down to the molten sea, with a few outcrops of solid rock on the shoreline. The Multi snagged on one of them, with lava waves breaking all around it.

The trailer broke free and vanished into the lava, whilst the wheels of the stricken Multi spun as power was applied in a desperate attempt to free it from the rock. It was rocking from side to side as the pilot tried to drive it off of the spear of rock that was holding him fast. We could see what he couldn't: the composite on the tyres had melted and they were now little more than metal mesh, gaining no purchase in the hot sand.

The movement must have weakened the rock as the outcrop suddenly collapsed, dropping the Multi so that the aft end was engulfed in the lava.

As we watched, unable to help, the paint on the hull blistered and started to blacken; of course it couldn't burn as there was no oxygen outside. The pressurised tanks of methane and air exploded, opening the hull like a tin can, just as the fore hatch opened and a figure crawled out, pulling themselves along the jib to the end. They made a leap for the shore, landing between the waves of lava.

Reaching solid ground they started to climb towards us, through the burning sand. Whoever it was had timed their leap well and got above the tideline in between the waves. They were followed from the hatch by another, who also attempted the leap; however their timing was not as good and the Multi had sunk deeper while they were climbing. They were overtaken by a crimson breaker, which engulfed them to the knee.

They stopped and threw up their arms, then sank down in a huddle as the next wave broke completely over them. As it receded, the beach was washed clear. No one else emerged from the Multi, which tipped up and sank into the thrashing waves, without a ripple.

We all wondered who the survivor was. Flanagan's radio broke the silence: "If that's Markes, she's coming with me," he said, although there was a murmur from Al and Tash. I wondered if he would be able to do it. The suited figure clambered over the last of the rocks and fell down at our feet, clearly exhausted and half boiled. Al and Tash went through the airlock; helmetless I couldn't help.

Between them they lifted the lifeless body onto the access platform. Tash came back into the cabin and started up the engine.

"Who is it?" I asked her.

"Dunno," she replied with a shrug. "The visor is covered with dust and it's darkened as well. Whoever it is is unconscious. We can't lift them in here, and there's not enough room anyway. Al is staying outside to make sure they don't fall off."

Just then an alarm went off. "That's the low atmosphere alarm," said Tash. "There were three of us in here for a while and the cab is only designed for two."

"Head for the lookout," I said as Tash pulled her visor down. We called Flanagan and set off for the lookout, with the alarm blaring all the way. We were on the last of the tank as we drove into the airlock, and I was starting to get a headache from the carbon monoxide build-up.

When we got through, Tash opened the hatch and fresh air flooded in. It had never smelt better. Not knowing who was in the suit, we took the helmet off. Al stood back with a metal bar in case it was Donna or Chumna. As the helmet came off we saw it was Hughie, drenched in sweat and with steam coming out of the neck of his suit. Tash fumbled with the seals to release him from its confines.

We lifted Hughie out and into a sitting position and Al went to get some water from the store. He returned with a bottle of Reevis water and splashed some on Hughie's face. Spluttering, he regained consciousness. "My head hurts," he said.

"How did you get away?" asked Flanagan, who had just come through the lock and got out of his vehicle. "I thought it would be Donna or Chummie."

"Chumna was driving. He was killed in the fall," replied Hughie. "He wasn't strapped in and I heard his neck break as we tumbled. I was suited and tied up in one of the seats, quite securely as it happens, and protected from the impact. I managed to free my feet and as Donna climbed to the rear to get her helmet I played dead as she passed me. All the safety gear lockers had burst open and a cutter was just in my reach, so I could cut myself free."

He paused and took a long drink of water. "It was getting pretty warm in the cab, and the plastics were starting to melt. I could hear Donna behind me; I didn't hang around to see what she was doing, just shut my visor and went for the hatch. The lock was jammed so I hit the emergency. I didn't know if her suit was sealed or not and to be honest, I didn't really care."

He took another long drink of water, throwing the empty bottle away. Al went to get another as he told the rest of his tale. "As I opened the hatch, I heard Donna behind me, but by then I just wanted to get out. She grabbed my foot but I kicked back and she let go. Once I was on the outside, I went as far up the jib as I could, then timed my jump between the surges of lava. Did Donna make it?"

"No," said Tash, and his face fell.

"I didn't like her but no one deserves to die like that. I was nearly boiled in my skin and it wasn't pleasant."

"She would have killed you," I reminded him.

"But that doesn't make it right," he said. "She should have been put on trial, and then faced the back of a cell door for a long while."

I shuddered; I knew what that felt like.

Lights flashed in the tunnel, more police had turned up. Flanagan went back into his vehicle to talk to them on the secure radio.

Tash was looking straight at me and I saw that one of her eyes had changed colour; a contact lens must have fallen out in all the bumping around. Now I could see her green eye, and the absence of dark hair made me realise that Donna was right; I had found her.

"You're Layla Balcom," I exclaimed and she nodded. "So who was Tash?"

"She was my alter ego. When I wanted to be part of Balcom, my father said if you're serious about it, go away and learn the business. I wanted to escape from people like you, no offense, and have a normal college life, so I called myself Tash Perdue. It's from an old Terran language; it means lost. She came in handy again when I hid out here."

"Someone must have known who you really were?"

"Harris knew, but no one else. I had to hide after I tried to warn my father about Donna. He was so besotted with her that he wouldn't have it, and she must have overheard us arguing. I found out that she had decided that I was a liability and needed to be removed. That's when I disappeared."

Al was stunned. "I never knew," he said. "Nic rambled something about having found you but didn't say where."

"That's right; he told me that he had got some interesting stuff from an immigration guy who was drunk. That was just before I went away last time. He wouldn't tell me what it was, just said he would have a surprise for me next time I came back."

Flanagan came back to us; he was smiling. "Right," he said, "I have explained to my superior what's been happening. Dome Control have been on to him – they spotted the chase and the unmarked vehicles. I've told him that Chumna was spying for Donna, that he was spying for Tony Hays from the police and that you were all caught up in it. Officially, you're all required for questioning, but not as suspects in the unfortunate accident." He turned to Hughie.

"Mr Wallsom, can you tell us the rest of the bad apples in Balcom? We can round them all up."

Hughie nodded. "Shelly Markes, for a start," he said. "She's the key. If you can get her then the rest of the management will fall into line, They'll all try and blame each other, we can weed them out at our lesuire."

Flanagan grinned. "Shelly Markes was apprehended at the port today, trying to get off planet," he informed us, "I just hadn't had time to tell you that yet." His mention of time jogged my memory.

"What's the time?" I asked. I had remembered the meeting in the research dome and Tony's threat. "Call Harris and check that everyone's alright."

"Why?" asked Flanagan. I told him of Tony's threat to destroy the dome. He got on the police radio straight away. He was away talking for a long time, while we waited in anticipation.

"My boss has spoken to Harris," he said as he returned. "He said to tell you that the problem has been resolved, do you understand?" We all relaxed.

"There's going to be a stop on anyone else leaving the cluster until we've had a chance to check all the documents on the drive. A team of agents from the Federation will be coming along just as soon as they can get here."

"The stock price will plummet again," said Hughie. "What's your plan, Miss Balcom?"

She just looked at him. "Well?" he repeated. "Balcom won't run itself, what's your plan?"

"You're in charge now, Tash...I mean, Layla," I told her.

"Don't be daft," she put her arms round me, "I'm Tash Perdue, freelance prospector, and what's happening in Balcom is really the least of my worries."

I smiled. "In case you hadn't noticed, you haven't got a prospecting rig anymore." Her face fell. "Anyway you won't have time for that; you're the lady in charge now that Donna has gone. You can safely return to your rightful place in the management of Balcom."

Her face changed as she realised the enormity of what had happened. "I guess so," she said, "and this time we will be a different company, more like the Balcom of old. We will be completely honest in all our dealings."

She looked at me. "Of course, we will need a new press officer to help promote our reformed image. Do you fancy the job?"

For more by Richard Dee visit his website
www.richarddeescifi.co.uk

Lightning Source UK Ltd.
Milton Keynes UK
UKOW04f0651141015

260476UK00001B/3/P